one little favor for a friend . . .

I spoke slowly, to make sure he understood. "You say nothing matters any more. I hope you mean that. Because if you're determined to go through with it, I'm asking you to take somebody else with you. It won't matter to you, and it'll make *my* life a hell of a lot easier. Kill yourself if you must. But before you do—kill somebody for me."

Charlie stared at me horrified. He had to swallow a couple of times before he could whisper, "What kind of an animal are you?"

"That kind," I answered evenly.

"You can't be serious!"

"I can. I am."

Charlie looked as if he wanted to throw up. "I can't commit murder, Earl."

"Sure you can. Anybody who can kill himself can kill another person," I said harshly. "And Charlie, it'll be so easy you'll be amazed. He's an old man and he won't give you any trouble at all."

Victoria Silver
DEATH OF A HARVARD FRESHMAN
DEATH OF A RADCLIFF ROOMMATE

William Kienzle
THE ROSARY MURDERS

Joseph Louis
MADELAINE

M. J. Adamson
NOT UNTIL A HOT FEBRUARY
A FEBRUARY FACE

Richard Fliegel
THE NEXT TO DIE

Conrad Haynes
BISHOP'S GAMBIT, DECLINED

Barbara Paul
FIRST GRAVEDIGGER
THE FOURTH WALL
KILL FEE
THE RENEWABLE VIRGIN

Benjamin Schutz
ALL THE OLD BARGAINS
EMBRACE THE WOLF

Carolyn G. Hart
DESIGN FOR MURDER
DEATH ON DEMAND

Jim Stinson
DOUBLE EXPOSURE

Lia Matera
WHERE LAWYERS FEAR TO TREAD

Joel Helgerson
SLOW BURN

Walter Dillon
DEADLY INTRUSION

Robert Crais
THE MONKEY'S RAINCOAT

first gravedigger

BARBARA
PAUL

BANTAM BOOKS
TORONTO • NEW YORK • LONDON • SYDNEY • AUCKLAND

All of the characters in this book are fictitious, and any resemblance to actual persons, living or dead, is purely coincidental.

This low-priced Bantam Book has been completely reset in a type face designed for easy reading, and was printed from new plates. It contains the complete text of the original hard-cover edition.
NOT ONE WORD HAS BEEN OMITTED.

FIRST GRAVEDIGGER

A Bantam Book / published by arrangement with Doubleday Publishing Company

PRINTING HISTORY
Doubleday edition published December 1980
Bantam edition / September 1987

Library of Congress Catalog Card Number: 80–1126

ISBN 0-553-26226-2

Published simultaneously in the United States and Canada

Bantam Books are published by Bantam Books, Inc. Its trademark, consisting of the words "Bantam Books" and the portrayal of a rooster, is Registered in U.S. Patent and Trademark Office and in other countries. Marca Registrada. Bantam Books, Inc., 666 Fifth Avenue, New York, New York 10103.

PRINTED IN THE UNITED STATES OF AMERICA

O 0 9 8 7 6 5 4 3 2 1

1

The only way to have a friend is to be one, said Emerson or Shakespeare or the Bible or Ann Landers. Man's best friend in need is a dog indeed. *I* came through when that cretin Charlie Bates started whining *You're my friend, Earl, you're the only friend I ever had*. I got him what he wanted, I helped him. You'd think that'd mean something, wouldn't you? I could have kicked him out—hell, I could have refused to let him in in the first place, sprawled out in the hallway the way he was. In the hallway, for Christ's sake!

You've got to understand about the Broadmoor. It's one of those ultrachic apartment buildings with a $$$$$ facade and a very visible security force. You can look through the glass doors and see this posh lobby with original artwork on the walls. The people going in and out wear expensive notice-me clothing—no tee shirts and blue jeans at the Broadmoor. Of course, inside the apartments the rooms are tiny, the kitchens better suited to dollhouses, and the closets downright microscopic. But the address is right and the tenants who pay the extortionate rents are clearly on their way up. At the Broadmoor, appearances count. So how do you think I felt when I came home from work and found this slob sitting on the hallway floor and leaning against my door and breathing out enough whiskey fumes to make the place a fire hazard and burbling *Hi, Earl, it's your old buddy Charlie Bates come to visit?*

"How'd you get past security downstairs?"

"Gave the man my last ten bucks."

So much for the Broadmoor's security system. Charlie's getting by the guard somehow failed to surprise me—it seemed a proper climax to a week in which just about everything that could go wrong in my life, did. Murphy's law in twenty-four-hour operation. If Chicken Little had shown up just then squawking his message of doom, I'd have believed him. Charlie Bates on my doorstep just capped the week.

I knew why the guard had let him in. The guard then on duty was a sour-faced man who looked down his nose at everyone who crossed his path. Ten bucks wasn't enough to buy him off. I'd once offered him a ten-dollar tip; he'd looked at me the way a king looks at a worm and then turned his back and walked away. He'd let drunken, down-at-the-heel Charlie Bates into the building just to embarrass me. The guard resented me the way he resented all the tenants. I lived in the Broadmoor and he worked there and that made the difference.

One look at Charlie Bates was enough to tell the guard or anyone else that here was a grade-A, number-one loser. Charlie was one of those people you spend your life trying to avoid. He broadcast gloom and defeat wherever he went, Joe Whatsisface in *Li'l Abner.*

Nothing Charlie ever tried had worked out for him. The first time I ever saw him we were both fifteen and he was getting hell from a woodshop teacher at Peabody High School. Our buddyship began to bud when I slipped him some answers for a math test we were both taking; thereafter he attached himself to me like a shadow. Charlie was useful. He was good for running errands and he fought most of my fights for me. His first venture into high finance came when he was sixteen and he talked the local Mafia lieutenant into letting him write numbers at the high school. He'd just gotten started when the state lottery came along and took most of his customers away from him. I don't think another numbers writer in Pittsburgh was hurt by the lottery because the Mafia gave better odds than the state. But Charlie was wiped out in two weeks. Nothing improved after that; the pattern was set. Work, family, friends—one by one they all let Charlie down. His version.

The other version was that Charlie took and took and took and never produced anything in return. Two of Charlie's three fathers-in-law had financed a couple of his penny-ante business schemes only to see their money go straight down the drain. Over the years Charlie had hit just about everybody he knew for a loan or an investment at least once—and then wondered why he didn't have any friends left. He'd moan and mutter something melodramatic about suicide and shame some soft-hearted, soft-headed soul into advancing him a few more bucks. Charlie Bates was a taker, but not a very efficient one. You might as well invest your money in surfboards for Bedouins for all the good it did Charlie. The only reason I still put up with him was that I'd never let him take anything from me.

In retrospect I guess I'd have to say Charlie Bates served a purpose in my life. He was a reminder that we'd both come from the same slum background, that what had happened to him could just as easily have happened to me. Charlie and I had started dead even, but Charlie had collapsed on the first lap while I was still in the race. Whenever things went wrong for me, I could look at Charlie Bates and feel good.

That's probably why I let him into the apartment: habit. Normally I'd sit there for a couple of hours and marvel at the man's stupidity—he saw nothing, he understood nothing. Once he'd tied his shoe by putting his foot on my

American Hepplewhite chair and then looked like a wounded puppy when I'd yelled at him. The only thing Charlie valued was cash, enough cash to see him through next week. So I'd told him what the Hepplewhite was worth, and he'd treated the chair with respect thereafter. I'd added another dead bolt after that visit.

But that was normally, and things weren't normal for me now. I was in danger of losing everything I valued; I needed a stimulus stronger than anything Charlie Bates could provide with his usual moaning and groaning. I needed inspiration. An opportunity the likes of which I'd never see again was slipping away and for the life of me I couldn't think how to hold on to it.

I'm going to have to back up. Charlie Bates came into the story late, and when he did he changed everything for me. Without ever fully understanding what he was doing. He came at a moment when I was desperate, when I would have grasped at anything I thought might save my neck. Charlie Bates wasn't much but Charlie Bates was what I had. So I used him.

At least that's what I thought I was doing.

My name is Earl Sommers, and at the time I'm telling you about I was an agent with Speer Galleries in Pittsburgh. Speer's specialized in antique furniture but we handled other pieces as well—we'd recently started buying Chinese wall hangings, for instance. We didn't really have enough room for storage and display of such space-consuming items and old man Speer didn't even like Orientalia. But he had a nose for where the money came from, so we were in the Chinese wall hangings business. Why the Pittsburgh rich should suddenly develop a hankering to surround themselves with silken scenes from the Far East was one of those little mysteries you learn to live with.

Costly oriental curiosities had nothing to do with me, though. I was a furniture man, more specifically a chair man. I love chairs. But nobody at Speer's was allowed that degree of specialization, so like everybody else I had to know a little bit about a lot of things. I'm being modest: I had to know a *lot* about a lot of things. We all did. Speer's was a medium-sized outfit when compared to a giant like Sotheby's, but Amos Speer had built an international reputation for himself as a man you couldn't fool. He was not inclined to be tolerant of mistakes.

Monday morning I was late. I'd spent the weekend at the Ballard estate, cataloguing. The Ballard consignment was a rich one—incredibly good pieces, and lots of them. Henry Ballard had been an old robber baron who'd hobnobbed with Andrew Carnegie and the rest of them, and his daughter Alice had recently died at age eighty-six, leaving an estate full of goodies. The heirs were understandably eager for the auction to take place as soon as possible. The Alice Ballard estate was the biggest job I'd worked on in a couple of years, but the only time I could seem to find for it was after I'd put in my eight at the gallery. So I'd been up late Sunday night, I'd had trouble getting up Monday morning, and I was late getting in.

Nobody punched a time clock at Speer's, but everybody seemed to notice when everybody else came in. My office was just off the auction room, and I'd almost made it when I ran into Leonard Wightman talking to Peg McAllister in the narrow hallway that connected the offices.

Now Peg was a good ole gal, but Wightman was one of those horse-faced upper-middle-class Englishmen whose voices carry for twenty miles. Amos Speer had lured him away from Christie's New York office—not too difficult, I suspected. Wightman had been one very small fish there. But Pittsburgh didn't offer that kind of competition; here he was the only English-born porcelain expert in town. Wightman had been living in the states for ten or twelve years now but his accent grew more Oxbridge every year. His schtick was needling people while pretending to be a hail-fellow-well-met type. He especially loved slipping it to me. When he'd first learned where I lived, he'd informed me with great glee that Broadmoor was the name of England's best-known institution for the confinement and treatment of the criminally insane.

"Well, well, well," Wightman said when he caught sight of me. "The barefoot boy with cheek. Is that a worry line I see bewrinkling your ignoble brow? Been pushing too hard lately, old chap?"

"You want something, Wightman? I'm in a hurry. Morning, Peg."

"Morning, Earl," she said cheerfully. Peg was pushing sixty but she never looked tired or rushed. I wondered how she did it.

"In a hurry, the man says," Wightman whinnied. "To bring a little beauty into a philistine world, no doubt. Ah well, to that auspicious end let me not admit impediments. Hasten on your way, dear boy."

"Thank you," I said dryly. "Now if you'll just move your ass so I can get by—"

Peg's eyebrows went up.

Wightman didn't move an inch. I pushed by him and went on to my office. He waited until I was opening the door and then said, "Oh, by the way, old chap, you are *wanted*. The Speer has been roaring since dawn. 'Is Sommers here?' he cried aloud, and, alas, none of us could say him yea. Isn't it nice to be wanted?" Smirk.

"You really are an asshole, Wightman," I told him in lieu of punching him in the mouth.

Peg's eyebrows climbed even higher. "What's eating you today, Earl?"

Wightman didn't give me a chance to answer. "Guilty conscience, I shouldn't be surprised. Did you ever see such a *furtive* look?"

Peg glared at him. "I don't think that's the least bit funny."

Wightman's eyes widened. "Neither do I."

I went into my office and closed the door.

The phone was ringing; it was the old man's secretary, June Murray. "Earl? I'm glad I caught you. Mr. Speer wants to see you."

"So I hear. What does he want, June?"

"Something to do with the Meissen Leda. It wouldn't hurt to bring your folder."

"Do I have it? I thought that went on to the file room."

"Didn't you keep a copy of your evaluation?"

"Hold on, let me look." I did a quick search through my files. "No, I don't have anything on it."

June came close to making a tut-tut sound. "All right, I'll have a duplicate made."

"Thanks, June. Why does he want to see me about the Meissen? Porcelain's not my bailiwick—I was just standing in for Wightman one day when he was sick."

"I don't know, Earl. You'll have to ask him."

"I'll do that," I said grimly. "Be there anon."

I was looking through my files one more time when a voice speaking my name made me jump. It was Peg McAllister, who'd just stuck her head through the door. "Earl, what's wrong? You're all on edge."

"Now what could possibly be wrong?" I said sarcastically. "With all his love all around me?"

Peg stage-sighed. "I do try to be helpful and supportive to my fellow slaves, really I do. But sometimes one of them whose initials are Earl Sommers makes it ver-y dif-fi-cult."

"Sorry, Peg. It's just that kind of day."

"Whenever I have one of those, I admit defeat early and go straight back to bed. What was Wightman needling you about?"

"Nothing in particular—just needling for the fun of it. You know how he is."

"Unfortunately."

"Got to rush, love," I said. "Speer awaits."

"Then go," she nodded. "His bite is worse than his bark."

I mustered a grin and headed toward Speer's office. If anybody knew about Speer's bite, it would be Peg McAllister. She'd been with the old man longer than any of the rest of us, from the early days when Speer Galleries was a one-room affair showing a few select pieces of Federal period furniture. Speer had set up shop in Philadelphia, where so much of our good furniture originally came from. But so many had been there before him he'd had to deal in pewter and glassware and portraits and the like just to make a go of it. Then one year he paid a bundle for a set of Revere tableware he later learned had been stolen.

So he'd hired Peg McAllister, fresh out of law school and totally ignorant of antiques. But she'd learned. She handled all of Speer's legal affairs, but her main responsibility over the years had been to track down the legal title to whatever her boss was thinking of buying. Speer had never been stung again.

Speer Galleries gradually earned a small, respectable reputation, but Amos Speer wasn't getting rich. There were too many other small, respectable dealers in Philadelphia. So he started looking longingly toward western Pennsylvania. Why should all that nice Scaife and Mellon money go to out-of-town dealers? Wouldn't an on-the-spot agent be of some value? So Speer and Peg and the one agent Speer had working for him at the time (long since departed) had packed up and moved to Pittsburgh.

It had been a smart move: Speer virtually had the market to himself. The antique dealers in the area at the time had been the smallest of small time; what few good pieces they'd carried Speer had picked up his first week in town. And the money came in. Amos Speer was an international dealer now, but it was Pittsburgh money that had put him over the top.

Agents had come and gone, but Peg McAllister went on forever. She had *become* Speer Galleries, as much the institution as the founder himself. Peg had been known to tell Amos Speer off in no uncertain terms whenever she thought he was taking a wrong turn. She was the only one at the gallery who could get away with it.

God knows I couldn't. Especially not now, when I was so far behind in my work. The reason I was so far behind was quite simple: my work load had more than doubled within the past month. No explanation offered. Cataloguing the Alice Ballard estate should have been a full-time job, and there should have been at least three of us on it. But I was responsible for the whole thing, and every day some new smaller job came in that would steal time from the Ballard evaluation. I'd tried putting the smaller jobs off until the big one was finished, but every day Speer or his secretary would call and want to know what about the spool table, anything on the Peter Cooper rocker, where's your report on the Duncan Phyfe, how may spindles on the new Windsor chair. It wasn't that we were all overworked; we weren't. None of the other agents seemed to be straining unduly. Just me. I didn't like what I was thinking.

June Murray looked up from her desk when I walked into Speer's outer office. She gave me a mouth-only smile and held out a sheet of paper, a photocopy of my evaluation of the Meissen figurine I'd examined about a week ago.

"June, you're a lifesaver. I owe you one." I gave her a winning smile with no noticeable effect. June was one of those just-average-looking women who through unstinting effort make themselves attractive. She had to look good, being in frequent contact with purchasers of beauty as she was. So she was always perfectly groomed. Always. I was willing to bet she put on make-up to take out the garbage. No, on second thought, there wouldn't be any garbage in June Murray's life. I started toward Speer's door.

"Ah . . ."

I stopped and looked back at her.

"Better not, Earl." The tone was friendly. I took my hand off the doorknob and waited while she buzzed the inner sanctum. "Mr. Sommers is here."

I worked at keeping my face impassive.

"He says he'll be with you in a moment," June told me. "Have a seat." I sat down and she turned back to her work.

From where I was sitting I had a three-quarter view of her face, and I wasn't surprised at the little smile that kept playing about her lips. By warning me, she'd kept me from putting my foot in it. I was supposed to remember that, add it to my account of favors owed. But the very act of warning me had reinforced her own authority, had made me acknowledge how much more in the know she was than I. She had controlled my movement. Some folks are quite ingenious at finding ways of putting other folks down.

While others like the old ways of doing it: Speer kept me waiting twenty-five minutes. I didn't even have the door closed behind me when he snapped, "Did you bring the Meissen evaluation?"

"Right here." I handed him the photocopy and took the chair facing him. The Meissen figurine was on his desk, a deliciously dainty Leda perched on the back of her oversexed swan.

He waited until I was settled and then said, "Sit down."

The bastard. I'd been coming in here and sitting down without an invitation for seven years, and now all of a sudden he decides my manners need correcting? It was a junior executive's trick, designed to embarrass the other fellow and put him at a disadvantage. Speer deliberately allowed an awkward silence to grow between us. I looked at that carefully barbered face and that sculptured white hair and those manicured hands and that impeccably tailored suit and wondered what it would take to make that dirty old man fall on his face.

Speer pointed a long finger at the Leda. "It is your considered opinion that this is old Meissen?" His voice had a sarcastic edge to it.

"You're saying it's not?"

"I'm saying look again."

I picked up the Leda; it felt heavy enough to be old Meissen. Old Meissen was eighteenth-century porcelain that weighed considerably more than the nineteenth-century reproductions of the same pieces ("new" Meissen). I turned the figurine over and looked at the mark: crossed swords, so that was all right. If it had said "Meissen," ironically, there'd have been no doubt that this was the inferior stuff; "Meissen" was the mark used by a nineteenth-century factory that just happened to be located in the same German town that had produced the earlier, more valuable porcelain.

The figurine had the right greenish tint to it, ever so slight; the later porcelains were generally dead white. Old Meissen was carefully decorated, and this piece certainly was. Ornamental lace border on Leda's gown, a few scattered flowers in her hair. The feathering carefully detailed on the swan's powerful outstretched wings. The colors were okay—no maroons or yellow greens, which were nineteenth-century introductions. So far everything checked out.

Then I saw. Leda's eyes—they were blue. All the eighteenth-century Meissen figures had brown eyes.

"New Meissen," I admitted, and put the figurine back on Speer's desk.

Speer pushed the photocopy of my evaluation toward me. "Do you see one word about eye color in there?"

He hadn't even looked at the paper; that meant he already had a copy. Telling me to bring in my evaluation—that was a ploy to put me on the defensive. I read through what I'd written and said, defensively, "You know these reports can't mention everything about a piece. Mostly they're concerned with matters that might be considered suspect."

"And blue eyes aren't suspect?" Speer snorted. "Good god, Sommers, even the rawest neophyte knows to look for brown eyes in old Meissen."

I narrowed my own brown eyes and studied him. He was absolutely right: eye color was one of the first things you look for. It was such an obvious giveaway. So obvious, in fact, that even a furniture man knew to look for it. If I hadn't mentioned eye color in my evaluation, it was because there'd been nothing unusual to mention. Which could mean only one thing: Speer had switched pieces on me.

He said nothing, watching me figure it out. Daring me to accuse him, to provide him with an excuse to—to do what? *Careful.*

I decided. "I'm sorry, Mr. Speer, I don't see how I could have overlooked that. Porcelains aren't really my field—if you'll remember, I was just helping out one day when Wightman was sick."

"No excuse, Sommers. I expect catholicity in my agents."

"Well, then, I probably rushed the evaluation. I've had an unusually high number of them this past month. Not to mention cataloguing the Alice Ballard estate."

Speer's eyes were gleaming. "Are you saying you're overworked?"

Enough was enough. "Yes, I am. The Ballard estate should take precedence over all these other evaluations, but I've had one distraction after another to keep me from finishing the job."

"How far are you from finishing?"

"End of the week. It'd be finished now if I could have given it my full attention."

"This week." He seemed to think it over. "Sommers, if you can't finish it this week, I'll put someone else on it."

I nodded. "I could use some help."

"You don't understand. I'll put someone else in charge."

No fun in tightening the screws if the guy you're screwing doesn't know about it. I got the message, all right. I nodded curtly to Speer and got up to leave.

He pulled Wightman's trick of letting me get all the way to the door before throwing his last bombshell. "By the way, Sommers, something a little more in your line has come in. A Mrs. Percy has what she calls an 'early American' writing table she wants to sell. She says it's two hundred years old. Run out and take a look at it, will you? June will give you the address. I'd like an evaluation by five this afternoon."

Look at this writing table. Finish that catalogue. Jump through this hoop. As I sleepwalked out I could hear Speer telling June to get Wightman on the phone.

June handed me an address card without looking up from the phone. Mrs. Percy of the 'early American' writing table lived in Beaver Falls. An hour to drive there, another hour to find the house and make the evaluation, an hour to drive back, allow for traffic, then write up the evaluation. Half a day shot.

Outside I crumpled the photocopy of my Meissen evaluation into a ball and looked for a place to throw it. Not a wastebasket in sight, of course. I stuck the wadded paper in my pocket.

Back in my office I lit a cigarette and tried to think. The scenario had changed. At one time I'd been the fair-haired boy at Speer Galleries, in line for the role of heir apparent. Speer was in his seventies; he was going to have to step down before too much longer. Three years ago I'd arranged for Speer to find out "accidentally" that Christie's had offered me a good position in their New York office; he'd immediately countered with a substantial raise. Speer hadn't wanted me to go then, and I had no intention of leaving. I wanted to run Speer Galleries myself; I wanted it so badly the wanting made me vulnerable.

But now it was clear that what I wanted wasn't what Speer wanted. Speer wanted me out. And he was going about getting me out in a particularly nasty way—giving me more work than I could possibly handle, rigging the evidence. That little stunt with the Meissen Leda—Speer was inviting a showdown. But I wasn't accepting any invitations today. I decided I needed an ally.

I went into Peg McAllister's office and told her what had happened.

She was stunned. "You mean he deliberately substituted a piece of new Meissen? Earl, are you sure? Couldn't you be mistaken?"

I just looked at her.

She answered her own question. "No, of course you wouldn't mistake a thing like that. And Speer would never get two pieces mixed up. It had to be deliberate."

"Exactly," I said. "And why did I have to make that evaluation in the first place? It wasn't urgent—it could have waited until Wightman got back."

"You mean Speer set you up?"

"I mean Speer's *been* setting me up for over a month now. All those extra evaluations I've had dumped on me? I could have finished the Alice Ballard cataloguing by now if it hadn't been for them. So Speer just now told me that if I didn't finish the Ballard job this week he'd give it to someone else—and then he hands me a new job that'll take most of the rest of today. He's setting me up, all right."

Peg was nodding, disturbed. "Yes, he's quite capable of doing a thing like that. But he wouldn't do it without a reason. Why, Earl? What's he got against you?"

"I don't have any idea," I lied. "Personality conflict, I guess."

But Peg wasn't buying that. "Not good enough. There's a man who's been here ten years that Speer can't stand. But he'll never get rid of him because he's so good at his work. And you're good at your work, Earl. You must have done something to him."

"But I didn't," I lied again. "I don't know why he's out to get me. I haven't done a thing!"

"Oh, come, dear boy, think back," said an officious voice behind me. "Not even *one* little indiscretion to return and haunt you? Even the blessed saints themselves don't claim to be that pure."

I faced him angrily. "You have something to say, Wightman? This is a private conversation."

"Oh, I always have something to say," Wightman told us unnecessarily. "And if you want privacy, shut the door. The Speer just consulted me about your little boo-boo with the Meissen, and I am now in the process of riding to the rescue. The June-bug says you have a photocopy of your evaluation. I'd like it back, please. Can't leave our dirty linen floating about, you know—dreadful metaphor, I apologize."

"What are you hinting at, Wightman?" Peg asked with a touch of asperity. "Who'd want that evaluation?"

"*Spies*," Wightman hissed melodramatically. "If word ever got out that Speer's couldn't tell new Meissen from old, the clients would start deserting in droves." Pure bull;

Wightman was just rubbing it in. He held out his hand. "Your evaluation, please."

My evaluation. I remembered wadding it into a ball and looking for a place to—ah. I pulled the crumpled paper out of my jacket pocket and ceremoniously handed it to Wightman. The look on his face helped a little.

"Dear me," he said with distaste. "Must you be so violent? But scrunched-up is better than nothing, I suppose. Ah well, now the world can resume its orderly orbit once again. Peg, my love, when are you coming away with me for an illicit weekend?"

"When hell freezes over."

"How very original," Wightman murmured as he left.

"One of these days," I said, closing the door behind him.

"Not before I do," Peg snapped. "When will I come away with him! I'm fifty-eight years old and I've been with Speer Galleries since I was twenty-four. And he talks to me as if I were some giggling schoolgirl who feels flattered every time a man flirts with her!"

I waited until her indignation sputtered itself out and then brought her back to my problem. "Speer wants me out, Peg. He's trying to get rid of me."

"Then why doesn't he come right out and fire you?"

"You know him better than I do, Peg. You tell me."

She sighed. "Because he likes to hurt."

That was the right answer. We'd both seen it happen before. Three or four years ago Speer had gotten rid of an agent who wasn't as sharp as he should have been, and he'd gone about it in the same unpleasant way—putting the man in impossible situations, even turning the other agents against him. Then when he'd made the agent as miserable as he could, he'd dismissed him. I was sure Peg had seen it other times too, before I came to Speer Galleries.

"Seven years I've been here," I said, allowing an edge of bitterness in my voice. "I've built my reputation at Speer's. You think other dealers are going to take on someone Amos

Speer has kicked out?" The antiques world wasn't like industry, where noncompeting companies absorbed one another's misfits. A dealer's financial life depended upon his having a reputation for trustworthiness, and any agent who was considered incompetent or not quite honest or suspect in any way was avoided like the plague. If Speer fired me, word would go out over the network and I wouldn't find a single door open to me. The only defense I could see was to leave voluntarily before Speer gave me the sack.

"Maybe he'll change his mind," Peg said with a false enthusiasm.

"You really believe that?"

"Anything's possible, Earl. He might. Don't let it get you down—Speer could do a complete about-face before the week is over."

So that was going to be her line. Buck up, don't lose hope, things will work out. Notice how Peg did *not* offer to go to Speer and put in a good word for me? I studied the expression of sympathy on her face—it was genuine, I was sure, but it was the limit of what I could expect from her.

Peg had had a good life with Speer Galleries—doing work she liked, traveling extensively. And, as a sort of side issue, prudently outliving two husbands along the way. She'd once told me about Amos Speer's first ventures into the international market, how he'd sent her hither and yon to check out legal titles. She'd go into a country where she'd never been before—not knowing the legal setup, not knowing the language, not even knowing how to go about hiring a reliable interpreter. She'd loved it. Obstacles were made to be surmounted. Then about the time she reached the age when gallivanting about was starting to become a chore instead of a pleasure, Scotland Yard had formed its art treasures squad and started doing a lot of her work for her. Peg was a fixture at Speer Galleries and she owned shares in the firm; she wasn't going to do any boat-rocking for my sake. She was quite willing to challenge Amos Speer on matters she thought were important—but my future obviously didn't fit into that category. Peg knew which side her bread was buttered on.

I went back to my office, called Mrs. Percy in Beaver Falls, and told he I was on my way.

2

On the way to Beaver Falls I had time to think. The Leda I'd examined the week before had been old Meissen, I was sure of it. If Speer had substituted a near-identical nineteenth-century reproduction, then what had he done with the original? I immediately ruled out theft; there was no way he could get away with it. Where had the Leda come from? I thought back and could remember no name, only a lot number. Not unusual. Also not very revealing. Except negatively, perhaps: What if the owner's name was Amos Speer? Both figurines could have come from Speer's personal collection and I'd have no way of knowing it. That must be it; it was the only way he could pull off a substitution without having to worry about ugly repercussions later. The owner wouldn't complain because Speer himself was the owner. End of the case of the missing Meissen.

Speer had been quick enough to call Wightman in and tell him I'd misidentified a piece. There was no reason Wightman needed to know; Speer had simply wanted him to. The new fair-haired boy? My god, that meant that if I did somehow manage to hold on to my job, I'd end up working for Wightman. Almost as unsettling was the fact that June Murray had taken it on herself to tell Wightman I had a photocopy of the evaluation. That means she'd decided the percentages lay with him and not with me.

The street in Beaver Falls where I parked had seen better days, but Mrs. Percy was young and pretty. And harassed-looking. Her living room had what is euphemistically called a lived-in look—I could hear young children's voices in the back yard. Department store furnishings—that bland, no-statement style that's somehow more offensive than outright vulgarity. Mrs. Percy and her husband weren't collectors; they were obviously a young couple in need of money who'd decided to sell off the family heirloom.

"We hate to give it up," Mrs. Percy was saying of the writing table as she led me to the den. "My husband's father says it's been in their family for five generations that he knows of, maybe more."

I made some noncommittal noise as we went into the den. Even from across the room I could tell this one wasn't the real McCoy. But for Mrs. Percy's sake I pulled out measuring tape and magnifying glass and went through the ritual of examination.

The table was a good imitation of an American Chippendale-style piece. Clean-lined marlboro legs supporting an essentially sober top structure with oddly inappropriate rococo carved ornament superimposed on it. I opened the drawers, peered underneath, took a few measurements.

I don't like giving people bad news. "I'm sorry, Mrs. Percy, it's a reproduction, not an original."

The color drained from her face; that wasn't what she'd been expecting. "But Denny's father said it was over two hundred years old!"

Denny's father lied. "An honest mistake. It happens a lot—your husband's family probably had an original at one time, but somebody sold it and substituted this one."

Mrs. Percy wasn't ready to give up. She went over to the only bookcase in the room—in the house, so far as I could tell—and pulled out a paperback book, her authority on how to identify antiques.

"Look," she said, pointing to a picture. It was an exact line drawing of the kind of writing table that now sat in Mrs. Percy's den. Even the ornamentation was similar. The drawing was labeled "Philadelphia, c. 1770."

I nodded. "That's the one your table's modeled after. Mrs. Percy, you can call in another evaluator if you like, but let me show you a few things." I pulled out one of the drawers and pointed to the dovetailing. "Eight joints. A drawer made two hundred years ago would have only one or two." I laid my tape measure across the joints. "The joints are uniform in size and evenly spaced. This dovetailing is machine-cut. The 1770 table in your book would have joints cut by hand, because the machinery for doing this kind of work wasn't developed until the nineteenth century."

"Oh," Mrs. Percy said blankly.

I reached in the space left by the drawer and felt the exposed wood. "Circular saw marks. Same objection—modern machinery was used. Look at the screws holding the drawer pulls. The notch in the head is perfectly centered in every one of them. Machine-made. Everything about this table—the thickness of the wood, the width of the planks—it's all too uniform to be eighteenth-century. It's a good piece of furniture, Mrs. Percy, but it doesn't have any antique value."

Mrs. Percy was drooping visibly; she'd been counting on that money. "Then Speer's isn't interested at all?"

"I'm afraid not. I'm sorry."

She tried to put a good face on it. "Well, then, I'm afraid I got you all the way out here for nothing." She laughed nervously.

I smiled. "Happens all the time. Don't worry about it."

"Would you like a cup of coffee before you leave?"

I declined. Mrs. Percy was chattering to cover her embarrassment and disappointment. I half listened as I followed her out of the den and down the short hallway—when I saw something that stopped me cold.

A half-open door on my right showed me the foot of an unmade bed, a chest of drawers, and two legs of a chair on the other side of the chest. "Mrs. Percy, could I take a look at that chair in there?"

She quickly closed the door and gave her nervous laugh. "That's just a raggedy old thing I should have gotten rid of long ago."

"I'd like to see it," I persisted.

Well, why not? you could see her thinking. "I tell you what. The light's better in the living room—I'll bring it in there."

I got the message: the room was messy and she didn't want me going in. I nodded and went back to the living room. Mrs. Percy soon appeared carrying the chair, and a pleasurable chill ran down my back. If that chair was what I thought it was . . .

I winced as Mrs. Percy banged a leg against the wall. She winced too, but because she'd made a mark on the wall. "I've been meaning to get it reupholstered," she said vaguely as she put the chair down in front of me.

It was a fauteuil, an upholstered armchair with open sides. The gilded wood, the broad back, the elaborate ornamentation, the basically squarish silhouette all screamed *Empire* at me. Flattened, outsplayed arms rested on armposts that took the form of winged sphinxes. The faded dark satin seat cover was split with age. (Unimportant, since the material could hardly be the original covering. It couldn't possibly be. Could it?)

But it was the variations from the norm that excited me. The paneled back curved more than the strictures of the period permitted. A gilt ormolu mount hid a joint on one side of the chair; the one on the other side had fallen off years ago. That didn't matter—I was sure the ormolu had been added later by someone other than the man who made the chair. But what decided it for me were the legs. They were unusually slender but needed no supporting stretchers—indicating good strong mahogany underneath all that gilt. Legs that were graceful and light in a period that demanded massive, Rock-of-Gibraltar furniture. I was sure I was looking at a Duprée chair.

Duprée had been a French cabinetmaker who hadn't paid adequate attention to the politics of his time. Napoleon had wanted to surround himself with furnishings that suggested permanence and grandeur, to lend authenticity to his upstart regime. So he demanded classical motifs and anything else that could link him to the historic past. As a result most Empire chairs were heavy, stiff, formal pieces resembling thrones. Made for show instead of comfort. Duprée had been one of the first cabinetmakers summoned to participate in this artificial image-building, but when he didn't follow the party line he found himself out on his ear. Duprée had loved graceful furniture more than he'd respected the Emperor's glamorized view of himself.

Consequently there were no more than a dozen authenticated Duprée pieces in existence. Duprée had not been as popular in his own time as the lesser talents employed by Napoleon, and for that reason he hadn't been imitated. If the chair looked like a Duprée, the chances were it *was* a Duprée. I ran my fingers along one of the arms. If I was right, I had a small fortune under my hand.

"I'm almost afraid to ask," I said. "Do you have the rest of the suite?"

Mrs. Percy looked as puzzled as I'd known she would. "What suite?"

"These pieces were all made as parts of suites," I lied. "There should be at least four more pieces—three identical chairs and a settee or sofa. Perhaps a footstool."

Mrs. Percy shook her head. "It was my mother's odd chair. It didn't match anything."

"That's too bad," I said soberly. "We'd be interested in a complete suite. I don't suppose there's any chance of your tracking the other pieces down?"

She wasn't particularly disappointed because she hadn't really expected anything. "Not a chance in the world. Mom said she bought it at a second-hand store when she and Dad first set up housekeeping. It was just her odd chair, that's all."

That must have been quite a story, how a rare Empire chair came to rest in a second-hand store in Beaver Falls, Pennyslvania. "Too bad this piece of ormolu is missing," I said, not mentioning that I would take the other one off as soon as I got the chair home.

Mrs. Percy shrugged philosophically. "I didn't think it was worth anything. I think Mom only paid four or five dollars for it."

I sighed, like a man giving in to temptation. "It's worth a great deal more than that. Look, Mrs. Percy, I'll buy the chair from you myself. I collect chairs. I'll give you five hundred dollars for it."

"Five hundred dollars!" Her eyes were wide. "For *that*?"

I laughed. "For that. In spite of the missing ormolu, the chair's a good example of its kind. And I don't have one like it in my collection." Neither did anybody else I knew. "It's worth five hundred to me. What do you say?"

She was all smiles. "I say yes!"

I made out a check for five hundred dollars. Amos Speer would have paid at least three hundred times that. I knew of only one sale of a Duprée chair in my lifetime. The Louvre had bullied or seduced or blackmailed a small French museum into giving up its one claim to fame. The amount paid, if I remembered correctly, had been just over two hundred thousand dollars. But that was a good twenty years ago, long before the current boom in antique furniture. On today's market the Duprée would go for twice that, I felt certain.

"You don't have your mother's sales slip, do you?" I asked Mrs. Percy. "Then I'm going to have to ask you to sign a legal form. All it says is that you have ownership free of encumbrance—that you're legally entitled to sell the chair."

She signed. The five hundred dollars wasn't anything like what she'd been expecting for the writing table, but help keep the wolf from the door a little longer. I'd written "Duprée chair" in the space labeled description, confident that Mrs. Percy's paperback would contain no mention of this little-known cabinetmaker's work. I handed one carbon of the form to Mrs. Percy. Now it was official: the chair was legally mine.

"Want me to help you carry it out to your car?" Mrs. Percy offered.

I suppressed a shudder. "No, I'll send someone out here to crate it." It would have to be at a time when I was home to accept delivery. "Saturday morning. Mrs. Percy, don't move the chair back to the bedroom. And keep the kids off it?"

She laughed naturally for the first time since I'd met her. "Don't worry, Mr. Sommers. I'll protect your five-hundred-dollar chair."

My four-hundred-thousand-dollar chair. I said goodbye and went out to my car. When I'd driven around the corner I let out a yell of triumph that made an old man on the sidewalk jump.

A Duprée chair! You pay five hundred dollars for the privilege of *seeing* a Duprée chair. As far as its real value was concerned, four hundred thousand might even be a conservative estimate. I stopped at a drugstore and used the pay phone to call the packing and delivery service I'd been using in the past.

It was an easy enough procedure. Speer would send me on an evaluation, I'd buy the piece cheaply for myself, and then turn in a negative report. People who weren't collectors were easy to fool. I'd started dealing for myself when I first realized I was under consideration as the eventual director of Speer Galleries. Such appointments carry certain perks, such as being allowed to buy a slice of the business. A small slice, in my case—more like a sliver. But even a [illegible] would take more funds than I could beg or borrow. So [illegible]llicit dealing was helping build up the old bank bal- [illegible] that it would matter now; my fair-haired-boy days [illegible] Not all the china in China would get me a piece of Speer Galleries now. But a genuine Duprée for only five hundred dollars? Only a fool would pass that up. Directorship or no directorship.

I laughed all the way back to Pittsburgh. Amos Speer had sent me on what he thought was a time-wasting expedition and had handed me the find of my life. Of course, if he ever found out what I'd done, what I'd been doing for the past few years, I'd be over my head in hot water. I might even go to jail. But I always chose my sources carefully; people who had good pieces in their homes always got a straight report. But the Mrs. Percys of the world—well, they were ripe for the picking. I couldn't even feel sorry for them. Mrs. Percy had looked at that Duprée all her life and had never really seen it. She deserved what she got.

Tuesday started off better. I got in early, even though I'd been working at Alice Ballard's estate until after midnight. The cataloguing was coming along; and when June Murray told me Speer wasn't coming in that day, I was able to relax a little.

But not for long. When I first got in I'd found a note on my desk saying Hall Downing wanted to see me. Downing was Speer's personal assistant. His was a catchall job; he did whatever Amos Speer told him to do. The note bore yesterday's date and a time notation of 8:15 P.M. So I wasn't the only one who'd worked late last night.

You don't go running after lackeys in any business, so I pushed the note aside and got down to what I'd come in early for, which was a session with Eckhardt's *Pennsylvania Clocks and Clockmakers*. Alice Ballard had had a clock that I was fairly sure was late seventeenth-century, but with things the way they were at Speer's I'd better be damned sure instead of just fairly sure. She'd also had twenty-three other clocks, over half of which dated from the eighteenth and nineteenth centuries. And by her bed I'd found a lighted-dial digital fast and slow time-scanning deep-tone alarm with LED dimmer switch. Old Alice had been a lady conscious of time.

I got in almost a full hour before a tapping at the door interrupted me. "Ah, you're here," said Hal Downing. "I was looking for you yesterday afternoon, Earl. You weren't in your office." Accusingly.

"I'm allowed out once every week. What's the problem?"

"Didn't you find my note? I have to talk to you."

Hal's perpetual put-upon air irritated me. "So what's the problem?" I said again.

"It's the listings you've turned in for the Alice Ballard auction brochure. I'm getting it ready for the printer and—"

"But I haven't finished cataloguing yet."

"I know, but Mr. Speer wanted to get started on it. It'd be easier to show you than explain. Let's go to my office."

Hal Downing's office was a windowless cubicle in the middle of the building. We squeezed in behind a worktable and Downing started showing me the layout for the printed brochure. After a while I began to see what the problem was. Downing talked all around it, but what it boiled down to was that the format for the furniture section of the brochure had been designed for a much lengthier listing than the one I'd turned in. That left lots of white space. A certain amount of white space was considered classy-looking, but my furniture listings took up only a fourth of each page. That was wasteful as well as amateurish-looking and meant Downing would be in trouble if he let it go to the printers that way.

"Gee, Hal, that's a toughie," I said, not giving a damn.

"The copy doesn't fit the design," he said mournfully.

"Seems to me the design ought to be picked to fit the copy."

"Oh, Mr. Speer chose this one himself," Downing said in a rush. "It's one of the stardard designs provided by the printer."

"I can see that, but why so many pages allotted for the furniture section? How many pages are there?"

"Fifty."

I snorted. "Fifty! You might need fifty pages for Buckingham Palace, but for the Alice Ballard estate? Totally unnecessary. Just cut down the number of pages."

Downing looked as if he wanted to cry. "Mr. Speer insisted on fifty pages. He was quite clear about that, Earl. He said you loved writing up furniture descriptions and could fill up fifty pages in no time. I *can't* change it—it's got to be fifty pages."

So that was it. Somehow this screwed-up brochure was going to boomerang back on me. I should have guessed it. Speer wasn't missing a trick.

I looked at Hal Downing. "What do you suggest?"

He picked up my original typed listings. "If you could just take it back and flush it out, I think we'll be all right."

A beat. "Do what?"

"Flush it out. Add more detail, expand your descriptions. You know—flush it out a little."

"How can I do that?" (With Drano?) "Everything that's pertinent is already in there."

"Oh, I'm not going to tell you how to do your job." Hal Downing could be obsequiously modest when he wanted to. "But you can flush it out a little, can't you?"

Did I have a choice? "I'll give it a try, Hal."

He breathed a sigh of relief and handed me the typewritten pages. Jesus Christ, a fifty-year-old man who didn't know the difference between flesh and flush.

But a sharper man wouldn't have made so good a lackey. This particular lackey had done his job and he'd done it beautifully, not even knowing he was a board piece in a game called Get Sommers. I went into the men's room, stood in one of the booths, and seriously considered Hal Downing's suggestion as to what I should do with the Alice Ballard furniture listings. No, better not.

The only way to get any work done was to stay away from the office. I told June Murray I was going to the Ballard estate and left.

* * *

I stayed away from the gallery the rest of Tuesday and all day Wednesday and Thursday. The cataloguing was pure pleasure; old Alice Ballard had gone for quality stuff every time. Well, almost every time. I'd done the furniture first, of course—pleasure before pleasure. But handling old Alice's things gave me a satisfaction I knew at the time was dangerous: I was allowing myself to be lulled into a peaceful state of mind when I should be working full time at finding a way to hang on at Speer's.

So the end of the cataloguing was in sight. I'd had to take a couple of hours off Thursday afternoon to tend to some personal business; her voice had been icy when she'd called the day before to find out where I'd been hiding lately. But by late Thursday night I'd finished the entire estate except for Alice's collection of glassware—which, fortunately, wasn't a big one. Glassware was my weak spot. I'd taken some pictures and made notes, and Friday morning I went into the gallery to check the reference books.

The first thing I saw when I sat down at my desk was a photocopy of the five-hundred-dollar check I'd made out to Mrs. Percy.

The room insisted on spinning for a full minute. Then it sort of wavered in a seasick motion for another five. When at last both room and stomach settled down, I tried to think what to do.

A photocopy. That meant Speer was holding the check itself. (Of course it was Speer—who else? The man you couldn't fool.) The check would be valid evidence in a criminal action against me. I couldn't even claim I'd not realized the true value of what I was buying—I'd written "Duprée chair" on the legal form I'd had Mrs. Percy sign, and Mrs. Percy had a carbon. Every antique furniture dealer in the world dreamed of finding a Duprée—I wouldn't be able to convince anyone I'd acted in innocent ignorance. If I'd met Mrs. Percy by chance and ended up buying her chair for a song, that would be one thing. But I'd gained admittance to her home as a bonded agent of Speer Galleries, and that made the difference between sharp business dealings and a felony. Speer had me right where he wanted me.

But how? How had he done it? Was that whole Beaver Falls scene just another setup? A trap—and I had just waltzed in, so bedazzled by the Duprée I hadn't thought to look out for tricks? But that would mean Mrs. Percy was in on it. Was she an actress Speer had hired as part of the con?

No; that was paranoia talking. Mrs. Percy was no actress, I was sure of that. No one who knew the true value of the Duprée would have handled the chair as casually as she did. No, it was more likely that Speer had gone to Beaver Falls himself to check up on me. And *that* suggested he suspected I'd been buying valuable pieces cheaply on the sly and turning in false reports on them. Easy way to find out; I located Mrs. Percy's address card and punched out her phone number.

All I had to do was identify myself and she started talking. "Oh, Mr. Sommers, how can I ever thank you! If you hadn't had second thoughts about that old chair—why, we would never have known how much it was worth! And they say there's no such thing as an honest man. I told Mr. Speer you could have taken the chair for five hundred dollars and we'd never have known the difference. He—"

"Mr. Speer himself was there?"

"Why, yes." She sounded puzzled. "Didn't you know? He said you'd been thinking about the chair and wanted his opinion."

"I've been out of town," I said smoothly. "I haven't had a chance to talk to him."

"Well, you were absolutely right about the chair—it *is* valuable. Three hundred thousand dollars' worth of valuable! I've never seen so much money all at once. Three hundred thousand for just a *chair!* I still can't believe it."

Three hundred thousand dollars. He gave that fool woman *three hundred thousand dollars*. Amos Speer hadn't gotten rich by being generous. Maintaining a reputation as an honest dealer forced him always to pay a fair price, but the prices he paid were invariably in the bottommost range of "fair." If he'd given Mrs. Percy three hundred thousand for the Duprée, that meant be expected it to bring in, at an absolute minimum, five. Five hundred thousand dollars, and I'd let it slip through my fingers. No, not exactly: I'd had it snatched out of my hands. Violently. By Amos God-damn-Him-to-Hell Speer.

"Mr. Speer said the chair was a real find," Mrs. Percy chattered on. "You know, at first I thought he was talking about the table—the early American writing table, remember? But when I showed him the chair, he got down-right excited."

I'll bet he did. The old bastard probably peed his pants. He had a Duprée and what he needed to hang me all in one swell foop. He'd gone there to find out if I was cheating him out of a valuable writing table; the chair had been a complete surprise. It was an opportunity handed him on a silver platter, and Amos Speer had never been one to pass up an oportunity. Or a silver platter. Mrs. Percy ran down eventually and I was able to say goodbye and hang up.

I'd been so cool, so sure of myself. And I'd botched it. At times the old man seemed omniscient—the man you couldn't fool. I sat there for almost an hour, trying to think of a plan. But all I did was succeed in starting a good, strong depression. Why didn't he send for me? When I couldn't stand it any longer, I reached for the phone.

June Murray answered. I had to clear my throat before I could say, "Is he there?"

"Mr. Speer won't be in today," June said formally. "Who's speaking?"

She knew damn well who was speaking. "It's Earl, June."

"Oh, yes. Mr. Speer wants to see you Monday morning, nine o'clock sharp. Don't be late."

"Yes, teacher," I said and hung up.

So I was to have the weekend to panic, maybe to dig myself in a little deeper. The old crock must really be enjoying himself. I needed something objective to concentrate on, to get myself clicking again. Alice Ballard's glassware collection.

By two o'clock I'd finished. I took my listings in and dropped them on June's desk. She raised a carefully shaped eyebrow at me.

"The Alice Ballard estate," I said. "The final listings."

June pretended to be surprised. "But didn't Mr. Speer tell you? Yesterday he assigned Mr. Wightman to finish the evaluation."

I turned and left without a word.

One more thing happened that day. Another of Speer's agents dropped by my office to tell me something. Her name was Robin Coulter, and the first time we'd met she'd looked at me with what I thought were bedroom eyes but what turned out to be just an accident of facial structure; she even looked at the pencil sharpener that way. She was married; but I hadn't thought that meant much and made my move. Mistake. Robin had never let me forget it. That Friday afternoon she came into my office and shut the door behind her.

"Aren't you afraid of losing your virtue?" It wasn't often I got in the first dig.

"Oh, I don't think you're any danger," she smiled with a deliberately artificial sweetness. "No danger at all." Unspoken: *any more.*

I pointed to a chair.

She shook her head. "I'm not going to stay. I just wanted to tell you I'm going to the Mercer auction next month. Mr. Speer decided yesterday."

It didn't hurt a bit. Not a bit. By then I was so numb nothing could have made an impression. For the past five years I'd been representing Speer's at the Elizabeth Mercer Gallery in New York. Mercer's was a smallish gallery that dealt imported furniture exclusively. Only museums and other dealers were invited to Mercer auctions; occasional exceptions were made, of course, but basically the auctions were in-profession affairs. No one from Speer's except me ever went to Mercer auctions—they were my special province, hands off, don't touch. Of course I knew by then I wouldn't be going any more, but myohmyohmy! How pretty little Robin did love telling me so!

She was looking at me with those falsely inviting eyes, waiting to see if I was going to pretend to be a good sport and offer my congratulations. Like hell I was. "Don't get mugged," I said.

She smiled, knowing she'd scored. "It was a surprise to me, Earl. A delightful surprise—but I wasn't expecting it. You must have done something really dreadful. What did you do, Earl?"

"I exposed myself to Speer's wife. Want to see how I did it?"

Robin laughed. "I knew you'd fall back on sexual insult when everything else failed. You think you're so sharp, Earl. But you're not. You're not sharp at all. You're clumsy."

I knicked the door open. "Get out of here."

She left. I slammed the door behind her and stood in the middle of the room for a minute, not knowing what to do next. I decided to get the hell out. Robin Coulter's crowing had been the last straw.

I drove home in angry fits and starts, gunning the engine, taking chances. I was scared. I was good as the next guy in a one-on-one situation, but Amos Speer was mobilizing an army against me—the antiques world, lawyers, police. It wasn't enough that he'd stolen a five-hundred-thousand-dollar Duprée from me; he wouldn't be satisfied until I was in jail for stealing from *him*. If I was going to protect my own ass, I was going to have to do something dramatic and I was going to have to do it that weekend. By the time I got home I was so full of hostility and anxiety and resentment I couldn't think straight. I just wanted to hole up and lock out the world for a while. That's when I found Charlie Bates lolling against my door.

I haven't mentioned Charlie Bates for a while—remember Charlie? Charlie the loser, Charlie the deadbeat, Charlie the suicidal jellyfish. Charlie Bates. Sprawling in the hallway outside my door, breathing out whiskey fumes and self-pity, babbling *Hi, Earl, it's your old buddy Charlie Bates come to visit*.

Go screw yourself, Charlie Bates.

3

"How'd you get past security downstairs?"

"Gave the man my last ten bucks."

"Well, get out of the way so I can open the door."

It took Charlie two attempts to roll over onto his knees. He struggled awkwardly to get to his feet while I unlocked the door. I didn't offer to help.

Charlie staggered toward the sofa while I went to the kitchen for a bottle of scotch and some glasses. I guess I was still hoping that Charlie's bellyaching might give me the boost it usually did. I emptied a couple of ice cube trays into a bowl and then poured myself a quick one. Charlie had a head start on me and I wanted to catch up as fast as possible.

I put everything on a low table before the sofa and sank into my leather chair. Charlie helped himself to a drink, babbling away a mile a minute. He was reciting a long list of woes with an easy assumption that I would be fascinated by this latest installment in his life story. Charlie Bates thought friends were made to be leaned on.

"I've had it, Earl," he was saying. "This is the end. This time I mean it. There ain't no reason to keep going. Nothing matters no more. I'm gonna do it. Nobody cares whether I live or die. I'm gonna do it."

I made a noncommittal sound, listening not so much to what he was saying as to the way he was saying it. Charlie had never even learned good English; he still talked like the slum kids we both once were.

"Earl, you're the only friend I got left. You gotta help me."

"How?"

"Get me a gun."

"Don't be an ass."

He protested, insisting he'd really reached the end of the line. He told me a long, rambling tale about how he'd just missed the chance of a lifetime. He said he could have had the East Pittsburgh franchise for a new fast foods chain but he just couldn't get up the capital. "Story of my life, Earl," he moaned. "Just one missed opportunity after another."

My mind began to wander—which often happened when I tried to listen to Charlie Bates for more than five minutes. Charlie's remark about missed opportunities had reminded me of one I thought Amos Speer had missed. Once when I'd been on a trip to Speer's London office, a woman who worked there had made a point of showing me what a few rare books had sold for that year. She knew about books and claimed we were passing up a gold mine by not handling them. When I got back to Pittsburgh I tried to talk Speer into it, but he was having none of it. Rare books involved a whole new set of rules, he said, and rare books specialists were a breed apart. I pointed out he already had one such specialist on the payroll and named the woman in London. But Speer was adamant about it, and so Speer Galleries still passed up the rare books market.

It was a mistake I wouldn't make if I were running things. Me, running Speer Galleries. What a laugh. I'd really thought I had a chance. I'd even made a good go at getting the funds I'd need to buy in. I stared at a chair across the room. It wasn't the Hepplewhite Charlie had once put his foot on; that had long since been sold for a nice profit. In its place stood a Phyfe lyre-back that could only appreciate in value. On the other side of the room was an eighteenth-century country cabinetmaker's attempt at fashioning a Philadelphia Chippendale side chair that I'd be glad to find a buyer for—heavy, thick-ankled imitator of its betters that it was. But in my bedroom sat a magnificent Seymour barrel-back of inlaid mahogany. I'd paid seven hundred for it and could get fourteen or fifteen thousand easy. It was a chair I should never have bought; I doubted I'd ever bring myself to sell it. Assuming I'd still be in a position to deal after Monday—an assumption that was growing more foolish by the hour. Amos Speer, bless his venomous soul, would soon see to it that my "career" as a dealer came to an abrupt and inglorious end. Maybe I could pick up Charlie's fast food franchise.

Charlie himself had started a new chapter in the ongoing saga of his boring, repetitive troubles. "You don't know the worst of it," he babbled. "Earl, I even owe the mob money. They're after me right now."

Whee.

"All that stuff about them breaking your legs if you don't pay? That ain't no joke, Earl. They really do that. They're looking for me right now—they're gonna bust me up and then I'll have a hospital bill on top of everything else."

I idly thought the mob must be slipping if they'd lend Charlie Bates money. I went into the kitchen to make some sandwiches.

Amos Speer, Amos Speer, Amos Speer. I sliced a round loaf of corn rye bread and thought about murder.

It was the only solution I could see. If Speer had already notified the police, I would have heard from them by now. No, Monday was the day the world was going to collapse. Speer was saving for himself the pleasure of telling me exactly what he was going to do to me. Monday morning, nine o'clock sharp, June Murray had said. That was my deadline. Accent on dead.

I took the sandwiches into the living room—Welsh cheese for me, baloney for Charlie. Amos Speer must be damn sure of himself to leave me the weekened to flounder through. Or sure of me. I tried to visualize the scene in which I killed Amos Speer. I tried it with a gun, a knife, the ubiquitous blunt instrument. None of them played. I could not see myself facing that old man and committing myself to an act that violent. I couldn't do it. At the last minute I'd chicken out, I knew it. It seemed to me murder must be a terribly intimate thing, the closeness between killer and victim like no other closeness in the world. I tried to think of myself putting my hands around Amos Speer's neck and squeezing. The thought sickened me.

If hit men just advertised in the yellow pages I'd have no problem. And there was a lot to be said for long-distance weapons like bombs. Plant the bomb and then detonate it by radio control—nothing intimate about that. I could handle that. I could push a button. But it was a little late to be thinking about bombs now.

Charlie was talking about suicide again, his mouth full of baloney in more ways than one. It was a surefire sympathy-grabber—announce you're going to do away with yourself and you're an instant object of concern. Suddenly everybody cares! Because I'd heard it all so many times before I didn't pay a whole lot of attention. I had my own problems.

"Listen at me, Earl," Charlie said when he'd eaten the last sandwich. "I'm through. This time I'm really up against it—there just ain't no way out. I'm gonna do it. Nothing matters no more."

"Sure, Charlie. We've all got problems."

"Dammit, Earl, I mean it! Nothing matters. Why keep going?"

"Drink up, Charlie. At least die happy."

Charlie made an angry gesture that knocked over my glass. "Hey! What'd you do that for?"

"I'm telling you I'm gonna kill myself and you sit there making jokes? D'you hear what I'm telling you?"

I got some paper towels and cleaned up the mess. "Charlie, it's the same tale of woe you've been singing for the last fifteen years. What's so bad this week that wasn't there last week?"

"Nothing. And thass what's wrong—nothing ever changes. I'm going nowhere, I owe more money than I can ever pay. I'll never get out from under. And it's always gonna be like this—nothing's gonna change for me. There ain't nothing to get up for in the morning, no reason to keep going. I don't even miss my wife no more."

"Number one, number two, or number three?"

Charlie got that hurt-puppy look. "Aw, Earl."

"Oh, come on," I said. "I didn't mean anything. As for the money problems, Charlie, let me teach you three magic words that'll put you in clover."

"What?"

"Stick 'em up."

And then Charlie Bates dropped his head into his hands and began to cry.

Great. Just what I needed—a blubbering suicide on my hands. "Oh, for crying out loud, Charlie, cut it out! Come on—stop it!" He pulled out a dirty handkerchief and blew his nose. "Charlie, have you ever taken a good look at yourself? Have you? Just look at you. You're always so *hangdog*."

"I know," he snuffled.

"You're so defeated-looking you tell every stranger you meet that you're a loser. Even before you open your mouth."

"I can't help it."

"And when you do open your mouth, it's always to complain about something."

"I got a lot to complain about, Earl! You don't live my life—you don't know what it's like. You're making good money, you're going places. But me—I'm never gonna get nowhere."

"Charlie, stop babbling."

"And they went and raised my rent. I can't even afford the rent I been paying! Everybody's got a hand out. And the inflation—y'know the cop in my neighborhood wants twenty dollars a week to let me park my car in the street now? Twenty dollars! I remember when you could park in that street for *three* dollars a week. Eighty bucks a month just to park that junk heap. Shit, Earl, the car ain't worth eighty bucks. Everything's out of hand. I dunno where I am anymore, I dunno where I'm going. It's just not worth the effort. Nothing matters no more."

Well, it went on like that all night. Charlie talked and talked and talked, as if he couldn't stop. I listened, and dozed, and thought about throwing him out, and didn't. The reason I didn't throw him out was that I was gradually coming to understand something. This time, I thought, this time it just might be different. This time I thought he really might go through with it—and the damn fool would do it right there in my apartment if I let him! I had my own problems, and here was this self-destructive slob sprawled out on my sofa complicating my life even further. But still I didn't throw him out.

Toward dawn I at last let in an idea that had been teasing at my mind all night. I thought about it and thought about it, while Charlie went on wallowing in self-pity. By the time the sun had come up, I'd decided to take a chance.

"Nothing matters no more," Charlie was saying for the ten-thousandth time.

I reached over and shook his shoulder. "Listen, Charlie, and listen good. I believe you. If you're sure this is what you want, I won't try to stop you. I won't get in your way."

"I'm sure. Will you help me? Can you get me a gun?"

I nodded. "I know where I can get one." From the right-hand drawer of Amos Speer's desk at Speer Galleries, that's where I could get one.

Charlie was so grateful he was disgusting. "Thanks, Earl, I knew I could count on you, you're the only real friend I ever had, I knew you wouldn't let me down—"

Yeah, yeah. "Charlie, how long have we been friends?"

"Since school. Uh, more'n twenty years."

"Twenty years is a long time. Charlie, all night you've been saying nothing matters any more. Do you mean that?"

"Course I mean it. God knows I mean it."

"Nothing at all matters?"

"Nothing."

"Not even life?"

"Not my life."

"What about somebody else's life?"

"What?"

"I said what about somebody else's life? Does that matter?"

"Whacha talking about?"

I spoke slowly, to make sure he understood. "You say nothing matters. I hope you mean that. Because if you're determined to go through with it, I'm asking you to take somebody else with you. It won't matter to you, and it'll make *my* life a hell of a lot easier. Kill yourself if you must. But before you do—kill somebody for me."

Charlie stared at me horrified, his mouth hanging open. He had to swallow a couple of times before he could whisper, "What kind of animal are you?"

"That kind," I answered evenly.

"You can't be serious!"

"I can. I am."

"I won't do it! I, I can't! Earl, how can you ask me?"

"Nothing matters, remember?"

"But, but you want me to *murder* somebody!"

"Are you afraid? Is that it? What'll they do to you? How can they punish you if you're already dead?"

Charlie looked as if he wanted to throw up. "I can't commit murder, Earl."

"Sure you can. Anybody who can kill himself can kill another person," I said harshly, sure that Charlie would never stop to examine the logic of *that*. "And Charlie, it'll be so easy you'll be amazed. He's an old man and he won't give you any trouble at all."

In spite of himself Charlie was curious. "Who is it?"

"His name is Amos Speer. He lives in Fox Chapel."

"Speer, Speer." Trying to place the name. "The guy you work for?"

"That's the one. He's out to get me, and the only way I can survive is to get him first. It's him or me, Charlie."

Charlie shook his head. "Uh, Fox Chapel."

I knew what was bothering him. Pittsburgh had a lot of big expensive houses squeezed right up against one another, but the people who lived in the Fox Chapel area of town could afford to surround themselves with land. Amos Speer lived on an estate. But Charlie was thinking about the problem, and that was a good sign.

"It'll be easy," I said confidently. "Saturdays Speer likes to work in his garden. His wife plays tennis every Saturday, regular as clockwork. No servants to worry about—some cleaning women and a couple of gardeners come in during the week, but on weekends only the Speers are there. The house has a security system—Speer keeps his collection of porcelains there. It's an alarm system that rings at police headquarters if there's an attempt to break in, and a guard patrols the grounds at night. But Speer won't be in the house, and you won't be there at night. You see? All you have to do is avoid the house. Go around to the back—Speer will be in the garden."

"What if he ain't?"

"He will be," I said with a confidence I wasn't really feeling. "Charlie, it'll be a piece of cake. One shot. That's all it'll take." I hoped I was keeping the desperation out of my voice.

Charlie was shaking his head. "I can't do it, Earl. I don't think you oughta—you shouldn't take advantage of me. Not now. It ain't right, Earl."

But I wasn't finished. "If nothing really matters to you, why should you balk at the idea of killing?"

"But, but this is different!"

"How is it different, Charlie? You did say *nothing* matters, didn't you? Didn't you?"

"Yeah, but hell—"

"Or were you just playing games?"

"Earl!"

"Trying to get your old buddy to feel sorry for you? Was that it? Was that it, Charlie?"

"No, no, I meant it. I—"

"Then prove it! Do this for me."

"Ah, Earl, don't put it like that!"

"Then think of it as a deal. I'll get a gun for you if you'll get Speer for me. That's fair, isn't it? Speer means nothing to you—you don't even know the man. But you know me—I'm your friend. At least, I thought I was your friend. Am I your friend, Charlie?"

"Sure you are, Earl. You know that."

"I've been your friend for over twenty years. Doesn't that matter either?"

Charlie looked ready to be carried out with the garbage.

"Doesn't that matter either, Charlie?" I persisted. "It does to me. Where else could you have gone last night? Do you know *anybody else in the world* who would have let you in?" He started crying again. "Even when you told me the mob was after you—did I kick you out? Did I?"

He ran his sleeve under his nose and shook his head.

"Charlie, did it even occur to you that you might be putting me in danger by coming here? Of course not. But it occurred to me—damn right it occurred to me. *But I still didn't kick you out*. You're here right now. Who else would do that for you? Who, Charlie?"

He lifted his awe-stricken face. "Nobody, Earl. You're the only one."

Once he understood that, I was halfway home. I kept hammering at him and hammering at him, and by the time the clock said 8 A.M., he had agreed to kill Amos Speer.

Charlie Bates was my long-distance weapon, my bomb. I'd primed him and put him on automatic timer. When the time came he'd self-destruct, and I'd be free of both Charlie and Amos Speer forever.

I drove Charlie to Highland Park and told him to go look at the yaks in the zoo. I'd meet him there as soon as I got the gun.

Good old Charlie Bates. All the time I kept telling myself I was crazy trying to get Charlie the loser to solve my problems for me. But an opportunity like this didn't come along every day. And I was running out of time.

The plan was simple. Charlie would take a cab to Speer's home, go around back to the garden, shoot Speer, and then shoot himself. Victim, murderer, murder weapon, all right there together in one neat little package. The cops would find out the murder weapon belonged to the victim and wonder how Charlie got hold of it. And there wouldn't be any clear motive for the killing, of course. But so many motiveless crimes are committed these days I was counting on the cops' thinking Charlie was just one more crazy in a world of crazies. I didn't let myself think of what would happen if Amos Speer decided he didn't want to get his hands dirty digging in the ground today. But whatever happened, I'd better establish an alibi for myself.

I drove to Speer Galleries and checked in with the guard at the door. The galleries used a combination of men, dogs, and computer-controlled electronics that made a break-in impossible, we'd been assured. (The insurance companies were satisfied.) I stood chatting with the guard for a minute so he'd remember me; I didn't want to depend on his written records alone.

I was just opening my office door when I heard a nasal voice say, "What's this? Another long-distance runner on the Speer treadmill?"

"Hello, Wightman."

"You surprise me, dear boy, you really do. Working on a Saturday. Even though Alice Ballard no longer sits upon your narrow shoulders. Such selfless devotion to labor is not a trait I'd have expected to find in your so-called character. Especially when the boss isn't here."

I didn't let myself rise to the bait. "Just a few odds and ends I want to get cleared up before Monday. But what about you? I thought weekends were your time to howl."

"And they are, O keen-eyed one, they are! Except that this weekend my fellow howler decided she really must go home to visit her sick mother—a story so patently flimsy I've already forgotten the poor girl's phone number. Now she'll never know what she's missed. I weep for her."

"Well, better luck next time."

"Never fear. Resilience is my middle name. Some of us are born to survive, don't you know."

"Yes, I know. Well, I'd better get at it if I want to get finished today."

"Ta-ta. Don't strain yourself, dear boy."

That was a stroke of luck, running into Wightman—much better than depending on the guard's records alone. Wightman was the perfect alibi. No one would ever suspect *him* of lying to protect me.

I waited until Wightman was in his own office, right down the hall from mine. Then I moved cautiously toward Speer's office, some distance away—peering around corners to make sure no guard or dog was patrolling nearby. I went through June Murray's office into the inner sanctum and headed straight for Speer's desk.

I put on gloves before I got to work. I had to break the lock to get the drawer open, but I was able to do it without marring the wood. The gun was in a chamois bag, a .38 automatic with a full clip. I would have preferred a revolver. If the automatic jammed, Charlie Bates was fully capable of blurting out that his old buddy Earl had foisted a bad gun off on him.

I slipped the automatic into my pocket and left Speer's office. I made a point of making noise as I passed Wightman's closed door. He was quick to investigate.

And gloat. "Leaving? You must have been here all of fifteen minutes. Sure you aren't overdoing it?"

The man had all the subtlety of a boa constrictor. "Pull in your fangs," I said. "Forgot something. I'll be back shortly."

"Of cooouuurrrse you will," he crooned, and shut his door.

I told the guard the same story when I checked out, and then drove back to Highland Park. I found a place to leave the car and walked through the zoo, only half believing

Charlie would still be waiting at the yak pens. But there he was, locked in eye contact with a great shaggy beast that was finding Charlie Bates an interesting specimen indeed. I had to slap Charlie on the shoulder to get his attention.

Instantly the yak was forgotten. "You got it?"

"I've got it. Let's go."

In the car I made Charlie repeat Amos Speer's address to make sure he still remembered it. Then I handed him the automatic.

But Charlie had had too much time alone with the yaks: he was having second thoughts. "Earl, I don't know about this."

"You know, in a way I envy you," I said quickly. "You're taking decisive action to end an intolerable situation. Not many people have the guts to do that."

"Yeah, well—"

"But at the same time—look, Charlie, why don't you take a week to think it over? You might change your mind."

"Uh."

"In a week you might think of another way to solve your problems. Who knows? You might find a way to pay off your debts. You might even score big. Maybe your wife will come back to you. Anything's possible."

"None of that'll happen."

"Miracles have happened before—"

"Not to me, they haven't."

"But maybe your luck's due to change. You might even win a new car on a quiz show—"

"Ha! Fat chance."

"You don't know, Charlie, you might—"

"Earl. You promised you wouldn't try'n stop me."

I let a long pause develop as I pretended to think about it. "Yes, I did say that, didn't I? All right, Charlie, I'll keep my word. I won't try to talk you out of it. Tell me Speer's address again."

He repeated it obediently. By now his death and Speer's were so linked in his mind that one presupposed the other. I drove him to a taxi stand on Bellefonte Street and handed him enough cash to pay the driver. He closed the car door and then stuck his head through the window.

"You're a real friend, Earl—the only friend I ever had." He stuck out his hand. "Goodbye, Earl."

I shook his hand. "Goodbye, Charlie."

He climbed into a cab. I watched his sad face looking at me through the rear window until the cab pulled around a corner and out of sight.

I risked a traffic ticket getting back to the gallery in a hurry. The guard wrote down 11:09 when I checked in. I banged on Wightman's door as I passed. "I'm back, you asshole!" A muted whinny answered me.

Then I settled down in my office to wait, hoping Wightman wouldn't be leaving soon. I got my wish. I sat there and twiddled my thumbs for *six hours*. About two o'clock my stomach started growling, but Wightman was either skipping lunch or he'd brought a sandwich with him. Another problem: lack of sleep was catching up with me, but I didn't dare let myself nod off. At a little before five I finally heard Wightman's door. I caught up with him and we checked out together. The same guard was at the door; now I had two witnesses to say I'd been at the gallery from eleven to five. I thought briefly of asking Wightman to have a drink with me to prolong the alibi but decided against it. That would have been so out of character it was bound to make him suspicious.

I stopped at a deli for something I could take with me and headed straight for the Broadmoor; I didn't want to miss the six-thirty news. I was starting my second Reuben when it came on. A sincere young woman gazed earnestly into the camera lens and intoned funereally:

> *Good evening. It's time for KOJW Newswatch. Our top story tonight is a murder in Fox Chapel. Amos Speer, owner of the world-renowned Speer Galleries, was found dead in his Fox Chapel home at three o'clock this afternoon.*

Wait a minute—*in* his home? Inside the house? The picture changed to show Speer's house and grounds. Then a series of confused shots of police moving around, an ambulance parked by the front entrance, two men carrying something out on a stretcher. Out. Out from the house.

Police say the cause of death was a thirty-eight caliber bullet in Speer's right temple. The body was discovered by the victim's widow, Mrs. Nedda Speer, upon her return from the Allegheny Racquet Club in North Hills. KOJW talked to Mrs. Speer.

The grieving widow was still wearing her tennis costume, and she looked like a million bucks. Which was about what she'd cost: Nedda Speer was a good forty years younger than her husband. A man with Harpo Marx hair was interviewing her:

HARPO: *Mrs. Speer, do you have any idea why your husband was shot?*
NEDDA: *Why, ah, ah, a prowler?*
HARPO: *The police say nothing was taken.*
NEDDA: *I don't think anything was taken. He must have been frightened off.*
HARPO: *Can you think of anyone who'd want to kill your husband?*
NEDDA: *Please leave me alone.*

Shot of widow striding catlike away from camera. Back to sincere young woman in studio.

News of Amos Speer's death is expected to rock the antiques world. Speer established the headquarters of his antiques empire in Pittsburgh in 1948. Speer Galleries has branches in San Francisco, London, Munich, and Rome. Speer was seventy-five years old at the time of his death.

He was seventy-two. They never got things like that right.

Police say the murder weapon has not been found. In spite of Mrs. Speer's belief that her husband was shot by a prowler, police are looking into the possibility that Speer's death is the work of a hired killer. We'll be back after this message.

Well, wasn't that just wonderful. And where was Charlie Bates? There were supposed to be *two* bodies there, remember. Two bodies and the murder weapon. Instead there was one body, no murder weapon, and one very large mystery to be investigated and investigated and investigated and investigated.

Good old Charlie. Good old reliable Charlie. There was one thing about Charlie you could always depend on: If there was any way at all to screw something up, you could always count on Charlie to find it. And I'd set it up—me, Earl Sommers. Temporary insanity, that must be it. I must have been totally out of my mind to trust the matter of my very survival to good old Charlie Bates.

4

A man shouldn't go around saying he's going to kill himself if he doesn't mean it. It distresses his friends, disappoints his enemies, and disconcerts the statistics-keepers. It also has a way of throwing a monkey wrench into other people's plans.

The television blithered away while I sat there alternating between cloud-nine ecstasy and snake-pit panic. Amos Speer was dead; that was the main thing. I could show up at the gallery Monday morning and go on as if Speer had never had me walking the plank at all. My aborted attempt to buy the Duprée chair for myself would not come to light, no tall man in a blue uniform would be reading me my rights, and my reputation in the antiques world would shine as pristine as ever. A definite plus, I'd say.

But then there was the other side of the ledger. Where the hell was Charlie Bates? What had happened? Charlie had pulled off the main stunt, which was getting Speer off my back. But then what? Had he looked at the blood flowing out of Amos Speer's right temple and thought *Ugh, there's got to be a better way to go than that?* Yep, it could have happened just that way. So then what? Had he just taken off to give himself time to reconsider?

And why was the body in the house? In the garden, I'd told Charlie. Maybe Speer had broken his usual pattern and skipped his Saturday session in the garden for once, but I found it hard to believe that Charlie would go into the house looking for him—even if the security alarm was turned off. It was a minor thing, but it bothered me.

The major thing, of course, was Charlie's whereabouts. If he'd just gone someplace else to finish the job—either with the gun or another way—then I could relax. But if he was wandering around out there somewhere, I could never relax. Not ever. He might be working that flabby mouth of his anyplace and god knows who'd be listening; Charlie just never knew when to shut up. Or he might show up on my doorstep again, whining *Earl, you're the only friend*, etc. He'd expect me to hide him, take care of him. Wear him like an albatross. And I'd have to do it, too.

I switched over to another channel that had a seven-thirty news program. It was mostly a repeat of what I'd already heard, the only additional information being that Mrs. Speer had said her husband was working in the garden when she left for her tennis lesson. Curiouser and curiouser. I turned off the set and reached for the phone.

Nedda Speer answered. "Hello?"

"Hi, doll."

"Earl. I was wondering when you'd call."

"Just now heard the news. Poor Amos."

"Yes."

"They don't know who did it—or why?"

"No, not a clue. It must have been a prowler."

"Guess so. But it's weird."

"Isn't it? A murder! Right here in this house."

"You holding up okay?"

"I'll make it."

"Listen, babe, one thing I want to know."

"Ask."

"How long a mourning period?"

"Oh, I think two months should be enough."

"Two months, right. Want to meet tonight?"

"I don't think I'd better leave the house for a few days. I'm getting a lot of sympathy visits."

"Call me when they stop."

"That I will." A door chime sounded in the background. "There's somebody now. Bye, lover, I'll call as soon as I can."

So that part of it was okay. Oh yes, that was another little thing I had going for me. I don't show all my hand at once. Nedda Speer thought I was hot stuff and I'd be damned careful not to do anything to make her change her mind. I didn't know which I enjoyed most—screwing Amos Speer out of valuable pieces of furniture or screwing his wife. Same kind of good feeling in both.

I didn't think Nedda would be too broken up by the death of her elderly husband. She'd long since decided Amos Speer was not the most exciting man on earth, so she'd gone shopping and she'd found me. Lately Nedda had been making it clear she'd much rather have me than creaky old Amos Speer living with her in the big house in Fox Chapel. That's why I'd asked her how long she intended to observe the forms of mourning. I hadn't even had to propose.

See what that meant? If Nedda didn't change her mind, I'd end up running Speer Galleries after all. Without having to put up one red cent. It was my ace in the hole, and it looked as if I was going to get to play it.

But Nedda could change her mind; that was the danger. She wasn't a very predictable woman. Sometimes Nedda made me uneasy; and sometimes she made me feel like king of the jungle. She had a pantherlike way of *stalking* me whenever she was in the mood that I found exciting as hell. I'd been going to bed with the lady for over three months but I still didn't feel as if I had a fix on her. I saw what she allowed me to see. And one thing Nedda allowed me to see was that she liked getting her own way; she may have wanted to marry me only because she knew she couldn't. But now that there was no obstacle in the way, she might well lose interest. She might look elsewhere for suitable marriage fodder, or she might decide not to marry at all. I was going to have to play this one very carefully; Nedda Speer was an opportunity I couldn't let get away. If I handled it right, I'd have it all.

Even the Duprée chair.

Monday morning everyone was walking around in a trance. They'd had all day Sunday to absorb the fact that their fearless leader was no longer with them, and now they were beginning to wonder what that meant in terms of their own lives. Robin Coulter, for instance, glared at me with open dislike. Without Amos Speer to say go, she was wondering if she'd still be attending the Mercer auction next month.

But Peg McAllister was actually trembling when I talked to her. "It's as if someone had attacked *me*, Earl," she explained. "Amos Speer and I were a team for thirty-four years. Now I've got this big hole in my life."

"I'm sorry, Peg. It must be harder for you than the rest of us."

"Thirty-four years! I've never worked for anyone but Amos Speer. I feel cut adrift."

I looked at her curiously. "You were actually fond of him, weren't you, Peg?"

She shrugged her shoulders. "When you spend your entire adult life working with the same person, you reach a point where fondness doesn't even enter into it anymore. I was used to him. He was part of my life." She paused. "He was *essential*."

Peg meant essential to her life, but I couldn't help thinking we'd soon see just how essential Amos Speer was. I didn't think he'd be all that hard to replace.

Speer's office had been taken over by the police, who were evidently not buying the prowler theory. We were being called in one at a time, and when my turn came a subdued June Murray ushered me into the inner sanctum.

"Earl Sommers, Lieutenant. Lieutenant D'Elia." Duh-LEE-uh. June completely ignored another man in the room. He was leaning against the wall, arms crossed over his chest, hugging himself. When June left the Lieutenant introduced him as Sergeant Pollock. Pollock inclined his head a quarter of an inch by way of acknowledgment but said nothing.

If it hadn't been for his name, I'd have thought D'Elia was Irish—stocky, sandy-haired, clear blue eyes. We shook hands over Amos Speer's desk. D'Elia motioned me to a chair and asked for my home address.

Then he said, "Let's get the nasty part out of the way first, Mr. Sommers. Where were you at two o'clock Saturday afternoon?"

"Here. Working." Two o'clock—about the time my stomach had started growling while I was waiting for Wightman to leave. I'd seen Charlie get into a cab a little before eleven. What had he been doing that took three hours? "You don't think it was a burglar Speer walked in on, then."

"We don't know what to think yet," the Lieutenant said. "But we have to check everybody. Do you have a key to the gallery or do you check in with a guard?"

"Check in with the guard. Even Mr. Speer had to check in—the insurance company insisted on it."

D'Elia nodded. "The guard keeps records of everyone coming in and going out?"

"Yes."

"Save me a little time. When did you check in?"

"I actually checked in twice. The first time was, oh, around ten o'clock. Then I remembered I'd left a file at home that I needed and went back for it. I got back here about an hour later."

"Anyone else working Saturday?"

"Leonard Wightman. He was already here when I checked in the first time, and we left together. About five o'clock."

"Did either of you go out for lunch?"

"No. I brought a sandwich with me." Might sound funny if I hadn't.

"You're sure Wightman didn't go out?"

"I'd have heard his door. His office is near mine. But the security guard's records will tell you whether he stayed in or not."

D'Elia paused. Then: "Is there a way of getting out of this building without being spotted by a guard?"

"None. It's tight as a drum." Then his implication hit me. "What are you saying? That Wightman or I sneaked out—"

"Relax, Mr. Sommers. We're still grasping at straws at this stage. You're one straw. The last person I talked to is another straw. The person I talk to next will be still another. We have to check everything."

The telephone saved me from having to think up a neutral reply. Lieutenant D'Elia picked up the receiver, said "Hello?", punched a button, said "Hello?" again. Pause. "Of course, have her come in."

The door opened and Nedda Speer walked in. This was the first time I'd seen her since last Thursday afternoon, when I'd stolen a few hours from cataloguing old Alice Ballard's estate for a different kind of pleasure. Sergeant Pollock unfolded himself from the wall and wordlessly placed a chair for her before the desk. Nedda nodded to me impersonally as she sat down.

"I'm sorry to break in on you, Lieutenant," she said, "but there's something you should know about. I've just discovered something was taken from the house after all. A porcelain figurine is missing, a valuable one."

"How valuable?"

"I can't put a dollar figure on it—Mr. Wightman could probably tell you. But it was in a case with seven other figurines—all of them were valuable. But only one was taken."

Lieutenant D'Elia was nodding thoughtfully. "That puts a different cast on it. Your husband could have surprised a burglar who shot him and then panicked and ran—I'm sorry, Mrs. Speer, I know this can't be easy for you. Can we get you something?"

Nedda was looking distressed. Immediately I was on my feet, offering to play errand boy, beating out Sergeant Pollock.

She waved a hand in my direction. "I'm all right. I'd like you to stay, Mr. Sommers. I need to ask you something."

I sat back down. I'd wanted to get out of the room because I was having a hell of a time keeping myself from grinning like an ape. I had no idea what Charlie'd thought he was doing when he took *one* piece of porcelain from the case. But it was the touch that was needed to make interrupted burglary seem a reasonable explanation. I didn't for one minute credit Charlie with thinking that far ahead—he didn't have the brains. But whatever his reasons, for once in his life Charlie Bates had managed to do something right.

"Bit unusual though," Lieutenant D'Elia was saying. "Thieves who go after paintings and jewelry and art objects almost never carry weapons. Most of them are afraid of guns. But then that would explain why this guy panicked and ran—maybe he'd never fired a gun before. Maybe it didn't belong to him—Mrs. Speer, did your husband keep a gun in the house?"

"No, Amos never owned a gun."

So Nedda hadn't known about the automatic the dear departed had kept in his office. Interesting.

Lieutenant D'Elia said, "I'd like Sergeant Pollock to take a look at the cabinet the porcelain was taken from. And then you could give him a description of the missing figurine."

"Certainly," Nedda said. Sergeant Pollock was standing at attention, ready to go. "But there's something I have to take care of first." She turned to me. "Mr. Sommers, I need someone to run the galleries until I can decide what I want to do. It's an imposition, I know, but would you be willing to take over the directorship on a temporary basis? Just to help me out?"

"Why, of course," I said magnanimously. "Don't worry about the galleries, Mrs. Speer. We'll take care of everything here."

She actually managed to look relieved. "Thank you," she said simply. "I'll talk to you again later—after the funeral, I suppose." Nedda stood up, catlike even in that movement. "Goodbye, Lieutenant. I'll let you get back to your investigation." Sergeant Pollock opened the door and followed her out; I still hadn't heard the man's voice.

"Attractive woman," Lieutenant D'Elia mused. "I suppose you know she's the sole heir."

"I'd assumed she was."

"Did she and Speer get along all right?"

"So far as I know."

"No trouble in the marriage? Amos Speer was a great deal older than his wife."

"I didn't know them socially, Lieutenant," I said, "but I don't think there was any trouble. Why don't you ask Peg McAllister? She knew Speer longer than any of us."

"I already did," D'Elia smiled, but offered no information. "I just realized I'm sitting at your desk—since you've just been promoted. Is there another room I can use?"

"No need. I have some work to finish up in my own office first. I won't be ready to move in right away."

"Fine. Mrs. Speer asked you to take over on a temporary basis. What's she likely to do in the way of long-term arrangements? What are her options?"

"Appoint me or one of the other agents or one of the branch managers as permanent director. Hire somebody from outside. Sell the business." I didn't mention the one possibility I was worried about: that Nedda would decide to run the galleries herself.

"Would you take the job on a permanent basis?" Lieutenant D'Elia asked me.

"Like a shot," I grinned. "Any of us would. It's a good business, Lieutenant. Running Speer Galleries is a job a lot of people would like to have."

"Well, you seem to have your foot in the door. Good luck. Was Speer on bad terms with anybody here at the gallery?"

My throat tightened. "I don't think so."

"Was he an easy man to work for?"

Aha, an out. "No, he wasn't. He was exacting and demanding and at times autocratic."

"And that didn't cause bad feeling?"

"Fleetingly. One thing you should understand, Lieutenant. Speer may not have been a boy scout, but he was a damned good dealer. For an antiques agent, the most important thing in the world is having a head honcho who knows what he's doing. Speer knew. He was a sharp old man. He was high-handed and impatient and sometimes he'd get mad at this agent or that one—hell, we all got a little of that at one time or another." (That was my out: spread the guilt.)

"Hm," D'Elia said noncommittally.

"But it didn't mean anything. Whenever there was disagreement, it was always over professional matters, never personal ones. Speer just didn't allow personal matters to interfere with the business of dealing." Then I remembered something. "Peg McAllister was telling me just the other day there was a man here Speer couldn't stand personally—but Speer had kept him on for ten years because he was so good at his work."

"Who?"

"Don't know. Peg didn't tell me that." And then could have bit my tongue: I just recalled the rest of that conservation. I'd been telling Peg that Speer was out to get me. And now D'Elia would ask Peg, and Peg would remember what we'd been talking about, and . . .

"What about other dealers, competitors?" D'Elia asked. "Any enemies there?"

But I decided it was my turn to ask a question. "Lieutenant, why are you asking about enemies? Are you saying it wasn't a burglar who killed him?"

"I'm trying to say as little as possible. This is what police work is, Mr. Sommers. Checking details. We check everything we can think of and then we check some more."

It went on like that another fifteen or twenty minutes—the Lieutenant asking for details of matters that had nothing at all to do with Charlie Bates and what had happened Saturday afternoon. I answered him willingly, supplying whatever information he thought he needed. At last he thanked me for my help and said he'd be in touch later.

June Murray stopped me on my way through the outer office. "Congratulations, Earl. Mrs. Speer told me you were the new acting director. I'm glad." Big friendly smile.

Well, well. The percentages were back with me.

I picked up a cardboard carton from the packing room and headed for my office. When I'd put my personal belongings in the box, I sat down to wait.

All in all it hadn't gone too badly—except for that one dumb slip I'd made. Even that might work out all right. Peg just might not remember what we'd been talking about when D'Elia asked her who the ten-year man was that Speer had disliked so much. Or she might be reminded but not say anything. Or maybe I could say something to her—no, better leave it alone. The one other time I'd tried to enlist her aid I hadn't gotten anywhere. This was one of those times when silence was probably golden.

It was the middle of the afternoon before June Murray called and said the police had gone and I could move in. I shouldered the cardboard carton and tried not to grin all the way there.

June helped me put things away. I could tell she wanted to say something but she waited until I was settled before she brought it up. "Lieutenant D'Elia asked me if there was bad feeling between Mr. Speer and any of the agents. I said no."

Ah so, the blackmailing began. But this was junior-grade manipulating, June's specialty—like not letting me go in to see Speer until she'd first told him I was there. No problem. "Good girl, June, I appreciate it. I've got enough on my mind without the police finding out Speer and I were at each other's throats over a piece of Meissen." Bring it out in the open, Honest Earl Sommers, that's me. "Get hold of Robin Coulter and tell her I want to see her, will you?"

June smiled her way out. I leaned back in Amos Speer's chair and reminded myself to get the lock on the right-hand drawer of the desk fixed. It wasn't properly a desk at all but a table Speer had used as a desk—American late Sheraton, cherrywood, the apron fitted with drawers. Good piece.

The phone buzzed. "Robin Coulter's here," said June.

Should I keep her waiting? Naw. "Send her in."

Robin Coulter came in and closed the door behind her. She took two steps and stopped, keeping a distance between us. Her eyes were doing their bedroom trick, but her mouth was a straight line.

"Unpack," I told her. "You ain't going nowhere."

5

But she did. I had to send Robin to the Mercer auction after all, because my first week behind the cherrywood table taught me I was going to have to pass up some of life's little goodies if I wanted to hold on to others. The sheer number of decisions that had to be made during the day left me exhausted and "virtually useless" at night, according to Nedda. The long drive back from Fox Chapel every night wasn't helping. Nedda was joking, of course. I hoped.

By the second week I was beginning to get the hang of it, and my performance improved in both bed and office. The auction of the Alice Ballard estate went off with only a few minor hitches (and a greatly reduced catalogue); we made a good commission. In the office I found myself depending on June Murray more than I really cared to. June loved helping me through the transition—oh, how she loved it! Making herself indispensable. And she was indispensable, damn her; but I was going to have to wean myself before an unbreakable pattern was formed. June prided herself on being the perfect secretary, but I soon found myself wishing she were a little less than perfect. Just once, for instance, I'd like to see her come into the office with her hair mussed up.

About the first thing I'd done on my own was get rid of Amos Speer's chair—a modern "executive" number specially built to provide additional support for his back. But my back didn't need extra help; so I had a chair brought in from the showroom, one I'd long had my eye on—a Boston leather-upholstered armchair in the high-backed William and Mary style. The other chairs in the office were good but not rare pieces I decided to leave where they were.

I called the rare books woman in London and told her to start planning her own department. I wasn't able to give her the go-ahead just yet, I said; but when the time came—a couple of months, probably—I wanted her to be ready to move.

Then I called in our art nouveau agent and told him it was quite likely that after a few months we'd no longer be handling his specialty. Amos Speer had hated art nouveau every bit as much as I did, but he'd kept dealing the stuff because it brought in the bucks. Our new rare books department in London would take up the slack. I watched the art nouveau agent pale to an unhealthy color and then told him solicitously that I'd hate to lose an agent as good as he was and did he think he could be happy working in some other area? He said he'd need some time to think and I gave it to him. If he could adjust, fine; if he couldn't, tough.

Next I sent for Hal Downing, Amos Speer's lackey, and informed him his services would no longer be required. Flush it out, flush it all out.

Just how much I could do all depended on Nedda, of course. Amos Speer had assembled a rubberstamp board of directors and I was assuming they'd follow the new owner's order just a obediently as they'd followed her husband's. There'd be no attempting to wrest control from Nedda; she was the majority shareholder now and that was that.

Appointing me interim director had been a logical step, one a distraught widow would be expected to make. And she'd been smart enough to make the appointment in the presence of Lieutenant D'Elia. If she'd handed full and permanent control over to me right away, there'd have been a lot of unpleasant speculating going on. But until Nedda and the board made it official, I could take only preparatory steps. Like a royal consort needing the queen's approval for everything he did. I began to understand Prince Albert a little better.

But in this best of all possible worlds the best of all possible things was that Charlie Bates remained the little man who wasn't there. I checked his apartment, two shabby rooms in the East Liberty section of town, not far from the squalid neighborhood where I'd spent my childhood. His landlady hadn't seen him for a couple of weeks and wanted to know when she'd get the back rent he owed her. Never, I hoped. I kept watching the papers for items about suicides leaping off the U.S. Steel Building or unidentified bodies being pulled out of the Monongahela River, but there was nothing that sounded like Charlie. Since I hadn't heard from him, I had no way of knowing whether he was alive or dead. The police seemed to be accepting the interrupted burglary theory, though; so I told myself to stop worrying about Charlie Bates and just count my blessings.

Which were numerous and gratifying. One such: the Duprée chair, reigning in unrivaled splendor over the house in Fox Chapel. I told Nedda to arrange for round-the-clock security; one night-patrolman wasn't enough with a Duprée in the house. Amos Speer hadn't been able to bring himself to turn the Duprée over to the gallery's restorers; he'd wanted to work on the chair himself. An impulse I fully understood. He'd taken the gratuitous ormolu off the one side and had made a start at cleaning the wood, but there was still a good deal to be done. I was looking forward to it.

What I did not look forward to was the almost daily visit of that horse-faced Englishman I intended to fire the minute I had full control. Wightman was the one thorn in my side; plucking him out was going to be a pleasure on the orgasmic-delights level. Porcelain experts were a dime a dozen; I'd have no trouble replacing him.

Buzz, buzz. "Mr. Wightman would like to see you."

"Tell him I'm in Tibet."

Door open. "Ah, there you are, dear boy." And he'd be off and running.

Every day it was something different. I was sure Wightman stayed up late at night making lists of things to complain about. I knew damn well he never did this to Speer; what I couldn't figure out was what he hoped to accomplish with his constant needling. Didn't the fool realize *I* was the boss now?

One day he came in to report on a quick trip he'd just made to the west coast. Our San Francisco branch had rather excitedly notified me they'd acquired a small lot of original Canton ware, the kind made for "home" consumption rather than the inferior porcelain turned out for export. They'd wanted Wightman to come out and authenticate it, and I'd okayed the trip mostly to get rid of him for a few days.

Now he was back, bristling with equal measures of indignation and self-importance. He sat down without being invited and spread some glossy eight-by-tens on the cherrywood table.

"Chinese export," Wightman snapped. "Shipped by the thousands to Europe and America for the last two centuries. Not without value, of course—this particular lot has the not-at-all unique distinction of having been produced in the late eighteenth century. I'd say our enterprising San Francisco cousins have an excellent chance of selling the lot for almost as much as they paid for it. But why they should have mistaken it for true Canton ware is beyond my not inconsiderable powers of comprehension. The quality is so *dreadfully* inferior—if it were only a little inferior, perhaps one could forgive them."

He paused for breath. I waited for the rest of it.

"Every piece in the lot has that grayish body you find in all Chinese export porcelain. And this export porcelain was shipped without decoration—so the importing country could have it ornamented to suit local notions of what oriental porcelain ought to look like. Look at this one."

"This one" was a color photo of a blue and white plate. The border was decorated with that everlasting willow pattern. The center showed a teahouse, a bridge with two people on it, birds, more willow trees.

Wightman leaned forward and stabbed at the photo with his forefinger. "True Canton ware never pictured people on the bridge. Never. Sommers, not one of those brilliant people out there noticed that! They are incredibly unobservant—or abysmally educated, I can't decide which. When I pointed out the figures on the bridge, one overaged teenybopper said, 'Oh yeah, hahn, I forgot about that.'" Wightman spoke the last sentence through his nose.

He was waiting for me to say something. "Incredible," I murmured.

"And that's not all. They simply have no feel for quality in porcelain. They have some truly exquisite pieces—but they show them side by side with overpriced modern reproductions. And Sommers," his voice dropped to a secrets-sharing level, "they're even displaying three pieces of 1930 Satsuma."

Wightman looked shocked, and he had every right. Satsuma made in the twenties and thirties was chop suey porcelain—gaudy, gilded stuff manufactured in Nagasaki strictly for the tourist trade. It's the kind of thing that gave "Made in Japan" its bad name in the first place. I'd seen my first piece of Satsuma when I was five or six years old—a large vase somebody was using as an umbrella stand. Even then I'd known it was junk.

"Who's in charge of porcelain out there?" I asked.

"That's just the problem—no one's in charge. Our highly paid San Francisco agents scatter their energies wherever their whimsy leads them. No one directs them, no one checks up on them. The branch manager is a businessman who I'm sure does a marvelous job of seeing the rent's paid on time, but he doesn't know Celadon from Imari. Those people need someone to organize them, to teach them a professional approach. The opportunities we're missing out there are enough to make you weep."

Aahhh, that was it. Now it was clear. Wightman wanted to run the San Francisco branch. I told him the situation definitely warranted looking into and I'd see to it myself. That seemed to satisfy him for the moment; he gathered up his photos and left.

Had I misread an earlier situation? I'd thought it was the directorship of the galleries Wightman had been after—but maybe his goals had been smaller all along. Wightman's lusting after the San Francisco branch manager's job would explain the stepped-up needling I'd been getting from him lately. He probably figured if he made himself obnoxious enough, I'd give him the job just to get him out of my hair. I leaned back in my leather chair and laughed. That was so like Wightman.

I knew he was exaggerating the inefficiency of the San Francisco agents; I'd seen the books. Most of their profit came from porcelain—they handled pieces in the two-hundred-thousand-dollar range. Wightman must have been waiting for them to make a big goof. Their mistake about the Canton ware was the opportunity he'd been watching for.

That night I told Nedda—waiting until *après*, of course—what Wightman had said about the San Francisco branch.

She rolled over on her back and laughed. "He's wanted to run that gallery for years. Wightman's convinced the west coast is just loaded with undiscovered porcelain that only his sensitive nose can sniff out."

I nuzzled her stomach. "Why didn't Amos let him do it?"

"Because European porcelain is Wightman's forte—Orientalia's a recently acquired taste, Amos said. But I suspect the real reason was he just wanted to keep him here. Amos always had him check out a piece before he bought it for his personal collection."

Including the brown-eyed Meissen Leda that had caused me so much trouble, no doubt. "What do you want to do about that collection?" I asked lazily. "Sell it or keep it?"

"I thought I'd keep it." Nedda raised herself up on one elbow. "That's not going to bother you, is it?" There was a hint of laughter in her voice.

I lay back and closed my eyes. "It would bother me only if you said sell it." Suddenly I felt a warm body on top of mine, and we both forgot about porcelain for a while.

The next day Robin Coulter called me from New York. Before she left Pittsburgh we'd gone over the preliminary listings of the imported furniture Mercer's was putting up for auction; now that she'd had a chance to examine the pieces she identified the ones she thought we should bid on. It was the same ritual I'd gone through with Amos Speer.

But when we'd agreed on which pieces and how high she should go, Robin had one more thing to tell me. "Earl, they have something not in the preliminary listings you might want to know about for yourself. It's a box-shaped armchair that's been dated first half of the sixteenth century. English, made of oak. The side panels are plain, but the chair back and the front covering are carved—nice, clean lines, nothing ornate. All the original pegs are there, but no cushion. You know more about chairs than I do," she finished innocently. "Do you think it sounds like a good one?"

"What about the grain?"

"Gorgeous. And the patina's great."

My mouth was watering. In all my time of illicitly buying and selling Hepplewhites and Duncan Phyfes I'd never even come close to a chair like the one Robin was describing. I knew the kind she was talking about; owning one was a little like having your own throne. Robin would be bidding against museums for it—my god, it'd cost a small fortune. I was sweating as I thought about committing myself to that much; I didn't have Nedda's money yet. Should I gamble?

"Go for it," I told Robin. "No limit."

"It's going to go high, Earl," she cautioned.

"I know that, damn it. Get it for me."

"Right," she said and hung up.

I was so excited it took me a good ten minutes to settle down. I hoped Robin wouldn't chicken out when the figures started climbing; I didn't really know how good she was at an auction. If she got the chair for me, I'd give her a bonus. I was pleased with Robin for another reason. The innocent way she'd asked my opinion told me she'd decided to play neophyte to my wise man. That suited me just fine. I wanted Bedroom Eyes to stick around for a while.

Later in the day she called back to say the chair was mine.

One loose end tied itself up with only minimal effort from me. Peg McAllister had been explaining some new tax regulations to me. When we'd finished, she said, "Earl, Lieutenant D'Elia said something that surprised me. He said you'd told him that *I* said there was an agent here Amos Speer couldn't stand. I don't remember telling you that—it was private knowledge I shouldn't have passed on. When did I tell you?"

She didn't remember! I wrinkled my forehead. "Oh, four or five months ago. It was one of those days I'd let Wightman get my goat—I think I was muttering about how some people were impossible to get along with." A subtle change in Peg's facial expression told me something. "It was Wightman? Wightman was the one Speer couldn't stand?" I laughed: wonderful.

Peg smiled. "I guess it doesn't matter now. But Speer disliked him even more than you do. Once he said he thought if he had to listen to that affected talk or smile back at that wolfish grin just one more day, he might commit an act of violence."

"Wolfish?" I said. "Wightman always seemed horse-faced to me."

Peg laughed, long and hearty. "We're going to have to get our animal imagery straightened out," she gasped. "He's always reminded me of a bird—a vulture, to be exact."

So that part was all right too. Peg had not told Lieutenant D'Elia that Speer had been on the verge of firing me, and my indiscreet mention of personal animosities to the Lieutenant had not reminded her. So Peg and I were still buddies; we could sit around and poke fun at Wightman and no harm done.

It was only two or three days after that that Nedda told me the board of directors had confirmed my appointment as permanent director of Speer Galleries.

I took the news with all the George Sanders aplomb I could muster. "So isn't it about time we were getting married?" I asked her.

The wedding took place in the house in Fox Chapel. I thought it a bit tacky to get hitched in the same room where old Amos had kicked the bucket, but that's the way Nedda wanted it. She'd dug up a swinging Episcopalian priest to perform the ceremony. He'd driven up in his black Jag, downed three martinis before starting on *Dearly beloved*, and managed to say the word "God" only once in the religious rites he pronounced.

The house was packed with guests: Nedda's numerous acquaintances, most of the staff from the gallery, and a few people I'd invited to keep it from looking as if all our friends were Nedda's. Wightman was there—oh boy was he there. Louder and more Oxbridge than ever. Peg McAllister kept trying to shush him, but he just wouldn't shush.

The other guests were more subdued. All these furtive little glances kept darting my way, as well as a smirk or two. We probably should have waited a little longer, but I had a feeling these people were going to smirk no matter what. Nedda and I were going to France for our wedding trip, and the limousine to take us to the airport was waiting outside with our luggage already in the trunk. I was thinking it was time to make our move when Wightman proposed a toast. No one had asked him to, but he wasn't going to let a little thing like that stand in his way.

"To the happy couple," he neighed. "Long may they wave! May their lives be free of controversy"—he pronounced it conTRAvassy—"and may the great tradition of Speer Galleries continue unabated in its winning ways. Continuity is all. The king is dead—long live the king!"

Awkward, embarrassed silence.

Wightman's eyes grew large. "My word, did I say something? Profuse apologies, one and all."

"It's time to go," I said to Nedda.

The goodbyes started. Peg McAllister gave me a restrained hug and a tight little smile while every man in the place was taking advantage of the opportunity to kiss Nedda.

June Murray came up to me. "Do I get to kiss the groom?"

"Lightly," Nedda called over her shoulder.

June's kiss was warm and quick. "I'm happy for you, Earl. I really am. I hope you get everything you want."

Strange way of putting it, but I thanked her and looked around to see if Robin Coulter was planning to follow June's lead. No such luck. But Wightman was advancing toward me, a determined look in his eye. I knew what he was going to say; he'd been saying it every day for the last month. I was ready for him.

"Now look, old chap," he started out, "I hate to bring business into the nuptial festivities, but I must. Do you seriously intend to leave this San Francisco matter dangling while you're off cavorting around the South of France? I seem to have failed miserably in my earnest attempts to impress upon you the need for immediate, heroic action."

"Wightman, I'm sorry—I must have forgotten to tell you. Distractions of the wedding and all. I did look into the

San Francisco matter, and I'm afraid you didn't see the total picture. They have some rather unusual problems out there." I was careful not to specify what they were. "The branch manager is doing an excellent job handling them—he's done so well, in fact that I've raised his salary. Don't want to lose a good man like that," I smiled.

Wightman's mouth didn't exactly drop open, but it came close. "But the porcelain!" he whinnied. "They aren't handling the porcelain right! They don't *know* anything about porcelain!"

"Again I have to disagree. We have a man named Holstein out there who is well on his way to becoming *the* authority in the field." I was sure Wightman knew Holstein was fresh out of college and still learning. "As a matter of fact, I'm thinking about transferring him to Pittsburgh. Take some of the burden off your shoulders. You wouldn't mind a little help, would you, Wightman?"

This time his mouth did drop open. I left him standing there agape while I went to collect my bride. We'd be gone for a month or two; let him stew.

I pried Nedda loose from the arms of a man whose name I couldn't remember and steered her out the door. The caterers would clean up and the security guards would lock up. All we had to do was make our getaway.

"What on earth did you say to Wightman?" Nedda laughed as the limousine pulled away from the house. "He looked as if you'd dropped a bomb on his head."

"Just gave him a little bad news I'd been saving until the last possible moment."

"Oh? Like what?"

"Like don't be too sure of your job, old bean."

"You're going to sack him?"

"The minute we get back."

Nedda looked thoughtful. "You really think you should? I know he's a horse's ass, but the man is an expert."

I put my arm around her and drew her close. "So are a lot of other people I know. Nedda, don't worry. I know what

I'm doing. Now for god's sake let's stop talking business—I've got other things in mind."

She grinned. "You'd better."

At Pittsburgh International the collapsible tunnel you walk through from the waiting area to the plane wasn't working or something, and we had to go outside to board. I had my foot on the bottom step when a movement off to my left caught my eye. I looked toward the observation platform—and got the shock of my life.

For there on the platform, leaning against the safety rail, stood the last man in the world I wanted to see—none other than Charlie Bates himself. Waving his arms, bobbing his head, mouthing *Good luck* at me. Grinning, happy, carefree.

Good old Charlie Bates.

6

Hell of a way to start a honeymoon.

Nedda knew immediately something was wrong. I pleaded a slight indisposition and retreated to one of the rest rooms the minute we were airborne. When I got back to the seat, Nedda handed me some Dramamine. I took it; it gave me an excuse to lie back quietly with my eyes closed.

Just when everything was coming to fruition for me—that's the moment my old buddy Charlie had chosen to make his reappearance. He'd been smiling and wishing me luck—his intentions seemed benevolent. That wasn't the problem. It was his loose lip I was worried about. Charlie Bates's mouth would always be a threat.

What the hell did he think he was doing, showing up like that? Charlie was such an ass he could have thought I'd been worrying about him and would be glad to see he was alive and well. That was the *last* thing I wanted to see. Where had he been all this time? He hadn't gone back to his apartment; I'd checked. Somehow he'd avoided both his creditors and his own self-destructive impulses. Or maybe I'd misread the situation. Yes, that must be it. All that bullshit about killing himself—it had been just another Charlie Bates play for sympathy and I'd fallen for it. I'd believed him because it suited my plans to believe him.

But then why had he gone through with the murder of Amos Speer? It didn't make sense. If it had all been nothing but talk, Charlie would never have pulled that trigger—he would have ducked out the minute he was out of my sight. So that meant I was right the first time: he *had* reached the end of his rope and had fully intended to kill himself.

But something had happened to change his mind, and that something could only have been the sight of Amos Speer lying there with his brains pouring out. Charlie had gotten scared, it was that simple. It was nothing more than sheer wishywashyness that had made Charlie rewrite the ending. And put me squarely behind the eight ball.

If I had to name the one person in the world who could never be trusted to hold his tongue, I would say Charlie Bates without a moment's hesitation. Charlie was a compulsive talker, afraid to let a silence develop, afraid not to use every available second to sell himself. He'd say anything to hold your attention—like threatening sucide when he thought that would do the trick. And this was the man who carried my secret around with him. This was one punch I couldn't roll with; something was going to have to be done. Charlie wouldn't want to talk, he'd even try hard not to. But he'd never manage it. Sooner or later he'd shoot off his mouth and that would be the end of Earl Sommers. No, as long as Charlie Bates was alive, I was in danger of losing everything—Speer Galleries, the Duprée chair, Nedda's money. Nothing was safe. The more I thought about it the clearer it became there was only one solution: I was going to have to kill Charlie.

No long-distance weapons this time—I'd have to do the job myself. The thought of *that* made me break out in a cold sweat, prompting curious looks from Nedda. I'd have to locate Charlie, make my plans, and then somehow crank myself up to going through with it. I'd have to. It was the only way. Yes.

Once I'd made the decision I began to relax. Charlie had kept his mouth shut so far; I was going to have to rely on his keeping quiet a little longer, until I got back. That was the weak part of the plan: the fact that Charlie hadn't spilled the beans so far didn't mean he wouldn't be seized by an urge to confess tomorrow morning. But there was nothing I could do about that. I'd have to bank on his continued silence until I could make sure he was silenced permanently. So be it.

By the time we were approaching Orly I had experienced a miraculous recovery from my indisposition. We'd leased a villa outside Nice, and I gave myself over to one long period of self-indulgence. France was beautiful, Nedda was beautiful, and at times even I felt beautiful. There were days when I could forget Charlie Bates for hours on end. I tried not to keep thinking I ought to be back in Pittsburgh taking care of the one man who could destroy me. But walking out on the honeymoon would be an invitation to a divorce, so I concentrated on enjoying myself.

When we'd been there a month, I started dropping little hints that it was time to be thinking of getting back. Conjugal bliss was great stuff, but business was business.

Nedda didn't take to the idea too well. "Well, thanks a lot, Earl," she said in mock-sarcastic tones. "That says a lot for the trip."

I sighed dramatically. "Nedda, love, life with you on the Côte d'Azur is nirvana itself. But all good things must come to an end."

"Why?"

"What?"

"Why must all good things come to an end?"

Because I've got to go back to Pittsburgh and murder somebody. "I don't *want* to end the honeymoon, Nedda," I said, overstressing the difference, "it's just that I think I *ought* to be getting back."

"Quibble, quibble." Nedda didn't want to leave yet and that was that. We stayed.

Part of me (the irrational part) was glad she was being so inflexible. France had something to offer I just couldn't get enough of: its chairs. My god, the chairs! Beautiful, exquisite pieces that delighted the eye and fed the soul. We took a few quick trips to Paris and other places, and I made some incredible buys. A Louis XIV walnut fauteuil dated 1680. An 1850 cane-seated papier-mâché chair inlaid with gilt and mother-of-pearl. A pair of Louis XV waxed beechwood chairs signed "Nagaret à Lyon."

But the biggest find was a High Gothic throne chair dating from the fifteenth century. The seat had been replaced sometime during the last century, but the cresting was intact and the bookfold paneling on the front and sides was original. It would complement without matching the grand English oak box chair Robin Coulter had bought for me from Mercer Gallery. I told Nedda what we could sell this one for, how much profit we'd realize on that one—all the time knowing most of them would end up in the house in Fox Chapel.

Amazing how quickly one adjusts to spending large sums of money. My days of hustling Hepplewhites were over (thank god; I hate Hepplewhite). I could indulge what Nedda jokingly referred to as my chair fetish without worrying about the bank balance, without worrying about being caught.

When we'd been there a little longer, I tried again. "It's been six weeks now, Nedda. I was counting on staying only a month."

She gave me her innocent look. "Is that why we paid two months' rent on the villa?"

I'd been hoping she wouldn't remember that. "When we were circling Orly, we talked about it. We agreed to stay a month."

"Did I agree to that? I seem to remember being told we'd stay a month."

"Nedda, if I'm going to run the galleries, I ought to be back there doing it."

"Relax, Earl. The business isn't going to collapse just because you're not there. Or is that what you're afraid of?"

I didn't have a snappy comeback for that, so I let it drop. It wasn't just Charlie Bates now; I was beginning to worry about the business a little too. I'd left Peg McAllister in charge and I knew she wouldn't let anything happen. Still.

We took a drive to Avignon; there was a showroom there I wanted to visit. The selection turned out to be disappointing—until I came to a chair that made me stop dead in utter astonishment.

It wasn't French. Never in their most manic moments had the French produced anything like that chair. No, the English were going to have to take the blame for this one. It was a Regency armchair built by someone who'd flipped his lid over a fad of the times. The Regency period was a time of extremes—simplicity was fashionable but excess was admired once in a while in relief. The man who'd made this chair had opted for the latter. English Regency was the more graceful counterpart of the trend-setting French Empire style—the last two consistent styles before nineteenth-century mass production, mass imitation. Both English and French styles went ape on occasion, trying to outdo each other in ornamentation that caught a popular rage of the times: a fascination with Egypt and all things Egyptian.

So what we had here was an English Regency Egyptian chair that must have been an elaborate imitation of a French Empire Egyptian chair. A mishmash. I couldn't tell at first glance what kind of wood had been used; every visible inch of it had been either gilded or painted black. Sphinx-head handgrips, lion-paw feet, other ornamentation in the form of lotus leaves, scrollwork, sun-and-pyramid, chimeras, crossed whip and scepter, ankhs, winged lions, scarabs, ostrich feathers, wheat sheaves. The chair that had everything. Even the three-inch spindles gratuitously inserted into the shortened back were delicately carved representations of cats—sacred ones, no doubt. Incredible, utterly incredible. I was laughing so hard my eyes were watering.

"I have a husband who laughs at chairs," Nedda said amiably.

What a preposterous chair. It had a lovely silhouette—but who pays attention to silhouette with such a whizbang display of ornamentation to distract the eye? Such a pretentious chair, a downright ridiculous chair, a wonderful chair. I bought it, of course.

"Do you really think Pittsburgh's ready for that?" Nedda smiled.

"We'll keep it around a while for laughs," I said. "Then we'll look for someone with enough sense of the absurd to appreciate it properly."

Nedda finally agreed to return to Pittsburgh, but only when eight weeks had passed. She'd intended to stay the full two months all along. I mentioned earlier that Nedda was used to having her own way; now I had a closer view of how she went about getting it. By mild resistance, evasive action, teasing answers to serious questions. No direct lay-down-the-law confrontations. But we ended up doing what she wanted. Wasn't it Jeanette MacDonald they called the iron butterfly? Bad analogy, don't know why I thought of it; there was nothing at all butterflylike about Nedda.

The iron panther?

Two things needed immediate attention.

First, locating Charlie Bates. That meant calling in outside help. Much as I thought about it, I couldn't see any way around it. I couldn't find Charlie myself (I'd tried once before), so I'd have to use a private investigator. So if Charlie's body were found after I'd killed him, I'd be up to my eyeballs trying to explain to Lieutenant D'Elia why I'd hired a detective to find him. Therefore I was going to have to figure out a plan that made sure Charlie completely disappeared from the face of the earth. Think that's easy? Try it sometime. Anyway, I contacted a big agency that claimed discretion was its middle name and told them to find Charlie Bates.

The second thing was taking care of Wightman. I'd originally planned to fire him the minute I got back, but in France I'd had time to think about it a little. It would be more fun if I did bring in that bright young kid from the San Francisco office. Let Wightman squirm a little first. I'd give more and more of his work to the kid and then sit back and watch the countermeasures Wightman would be sure to take. Should be quite a show.

But I never got to see it. When I called the manager of the San Francisco branch, he told me the kid had quit to go work for one of our competitors.

Hell.

The detective's name was Valentine, and the head of Triangle Inquiry Consultants (what a euphemism) had assured me he was "one of our best men." Valentine was rather colorless in appearance, a man easy to forget—a requisite in his trade, I suppose. He was curiously soft-spoken and polite, even overpolite. Not at all what you'd expect in a private eye. But even his elaborate courtesy couldn't take the sting out of what he was saying.

"To put it in a nutshell Mr. Sommers," Valentine said. "We can't find a trace of Charles Bates. When someone drops out of sight, we usually begin our search by talking to his family and friends. But Mr. Bates has no family—even his ex-wives have all moved away. And you seem to be his only friend. We checked the police blotter, hospital admissions—"

"A man can't just vanish into thin air."

"True. But he can leave town. If we'd had his picture we could have checked airport and bus terminals. But as it is, you can't expect a stewardess to recognize a man from just a verbal description, especially if he's someone she may have seen only once two months ago."

"I told you I didn't have a picture."

"I know. It's unfortunate, because Mr. Bates seems to be one of those people who go through life without ever leaving their mark on it. Whether this is intentional on Mr. Bates's part or not, I'm sure you're more qualified to say than I am. But the fact remains that he suddenly stopped appearing in the places he used to frequent. And nobody knows why. His landlady says he didn't move out, he just never came back. She still has his clothes and his personal belongings."

"Did you look through them?" A useless question, but I asked it.

Valentine nodded. "Nothing there. And his neighbors barely remember him. I checked with the Motor Vehicles Bureau to see if they had a new address for his driver's license. No luck. His car has been towed away—the police say it was abandoned. Mr. Sommers, may I ask if you were close to Mr. Bates?"

"No, not really. We'd known each other a long time, that's all."

"Well, then, I hope you won't be offended when I say Mr. Bates led a rather shabby life. And an empty one. Three failed marriages. Short-term odd jobs to tide him over between get-rich-quick schemes that never panned out. Always just one step ahead of his creditors. It's a familiar pattern. From what we learned about him, I'd say it was possible—even probable—that he just turned his back on the life he was leading and walked away from it. People are doing that now more than they used to. They just get fed up—and take a walk."

Hadn't thought of that. "And you think that's what Charlie did?"

"It's a strong possibility. We can rule out accident and suicide. You can't die in this town without showing up on somebody's records. I'd say your next step is to go to the police and file a missing persons report. The police have access to sources of information all over the country. All I can tell you is that we are reasonably sure Charles Bates is no longer in Pittsburgh, unless . . ."

"Unless what?"

"Unless he's gone into hiding. A man can turn invisible if he really puts his mind to it. New name, new bona fides, new appearance. New life-style. Perhaps your friend simply doesn't want to be found."

I pretended to accept this explanation and thanked Valentine for his help. Charlie Bates could no more change his way of living than I could rearrange the order of the universe.

When the detective had left, I worked at coming to terms with my mixed feelings. My best-laid plans for protecting myself against the threat posed by Charlie Bates's big mouth were all worthless if I couldn't find Charlie. Valentine seemed to think he wasn't going to be found without police help, and I wasn't about to go to the police. So long as Charlie stayed lost, maybe I'd be all right. I didn't see that I had much choice. I was just going to have to learn to live with not knowing what Charlie Bates was up to.

Once I'd made my mind up to that, I yielded to an enormous wave of relief. I wasn't going to have to kill him after all. I'd sent him to his death once and it didn't take. I'd do that same thing again if I had to. But that's different from firing the gun yourself.

That's messy.

Buzz, buzz. "Mr. Wightman to see you."

"Tell him I'm in—"

Door open. "Ah, there you are, dear boy." He sat down uninvited.

"Have a seat," I said sarcastically.

"Thank you," totally unperturbed. "I came to tell you, old chap, that after this week I will no longer be on your payroll."

God damn him, he beat me to the punch. "Just like that?"

"Oh, dear me, no! *Not* 'just like that.' The whole time you were abroad tripping the light fantastic, I was busily establishing my new home away from home, if you catch my drift. I estimate that with diligence, fortitude, and a few hours of overtime I will have my present work load in tip-top condition by Friday, ready to hand over to my downwardly mobile successor, whoever the poor soul may be."

"Surely I'm entitled to an explanation."

"That you are, dear boy, that you are. Quite simply put, my reason for leaving is this." He paused dramatically. "I don't think you've got what it takes to run this business. In my fully considered judgment, within two years the once eminent Speer Galleries will be going to the dogs. And frankly, old chap, I don't care for dogs all that much. You're going to fail, and I don't wish to fail with you. There. Could anything be plainer?"

I wanted to hit him. "Something about rats and desertion comes to mind."

"Ah, but to call me a rat you must first call yourself a sinking ship—and that's something you won't do until the very last minute. Until too late, as a matter of fact. And rather than wait around for the inevitable eleventh-hour hysterics, I prefer to make my exit upstage center and make it now. You never fully appreciated the Speer, old boy, and you never had the percipience to learn from him. He was a grasping old pirate, but he knew how to run a gallery. You don't."

I didn't even try to keep the anger out of my voice. "I know it'll be hard, but we'll try to struggle along without your services. Even though we both know I can replace you in five minutes. In fact, why wait until Friday? Why not get out right now?"

"There, you see!" Wightman neighed. "The Speer would never, never, *never* have said that! But because I got you angry—which, I might add, I have always been able to do with an absolute minimum of effort—because I got you angry, your only thought was to strike out, hit back, get even. Shall I tell you a secret? Amos Speer didn't like me. Hard to believe, but it's true. But whatever he thought of me personally, he was fully appreciative of my contribution to the business—a distinction you will never be able to make, dear boy."

"Wightman, I'm curious," I said. "How did you get a new position without a recommendation from Speer's? What lies did you tell?"

He threw back his head and whinnied. "My new employer didn't require a recommendation. He's quite capable of recognizing value when he sees it."

"And who is this sterling judge of character?"

"Me. I hired myself. Say hello to your newest competitor—I'm going into business for myself. Since I was unable to convince you there's still gold in them thar California hills, I decided to mine it myself. Don't look for such high profits from your San Francisco branch hereafter. I fully intend to take your west coast business away from you."

The sonofabitch. "You can't do that!" I blurted out, stupidly. "You can't tell me you quit and you're going to take my profits away from me and then just calmly get up and walk out—"

His eyes gleamed. "Watch."

And he calmly got up and walked out.

7

I spent the rest of that day contacting porcelain experts I knew and ended up scoring zero. It wasn't going to be as easy to replace Wightman as I'd thought.

So I wasn't in the best of moods when I got home to find Nedda in a prickly tête-à-tête with Lieutenant D'Elia. Why was that cop talking to my wife behind my back? Not that Nedda would give anything away. She didn't know anything.

"Martini?" Nedda asked me. I tried to read the expression on her face. "Lieutenant D'Elia says he just dropped in for a little chat." The stress on *says* was ever so slight.

"A martini would be nice," I nodded. "Is there something I can do for you, Lieutenant?"

D'Elia smiled easily. "Just dropped by to offer my congratulations. Belatedly, I'm afraid."

Sure you did. "Thank you."

"Congratulations seem in order on two accounts. Your marriage and your directorship."

"Yes." No help from me.

"Here you are." Nedda handed me a glass.

I took a sip of the martini; too dry. "Did you offer the Lieutenant a drink?"

Nedda smiled sweetly. "No, I didn't."

"That's all right, Mr. Sommers, I don't care for anything."

I used Amos Speer's trick of letting an awkward silence develop.

D'Elia cleared his throat. "I was just talking to your wife about France. I haven't been there since right after the war, but it sounds as if a lot has changed. According to what Mrs. Speer says."

"Mrs. Sommers," Nedda corrected.

"Oh, I'm sorry. Mrs. Sommers, of course. In my mind I still associate you with Amos Speer. I'll have to stop doing that."

"Yes, you will," Nedda said without inflection.

I finished the martini and put down the glass. Fidgety.

"Speer, Sommers. Names are interesting," D'Elia was saying. "Take your first name, Mrs. Sommers. I don't believe I've ever met anyone named Nedda before. Was your father's name Edward?"

"My father's name was Philip," Nedda said. "Both my parents were opera freaks. I was named after the heroine of *Pagliacci*."

The look of sudden pleasure on D'Elia's face surprised me; I'd momentarily forgotten he was Italian. "Oh, *that* Nedda!" he said with a grin. "That's great—an operatic name"

"Not so great," Nedda said dryly. "You know the opera? *That* Nedda is faithless, she's cruel, and she's not very bright." She gave the Lieutenant her cold smile. "I don't like being named after someone who's not very bright."

For the first time since I'd met him, D'Elia looked at a loss. But he made a fast recovery. "Names are an important part of first impressions," he said, "and first impressions go a long way. For instance, when Mr. Sommers walked through that door just now, I had to remind myself he's no longer an employee of Speer Galleries but its director. I actually had to remind myself."

"Imagine that," Nedda said with an edge of sarcasm.

"Funny how an idea gets planted in your head and you can't get it out."

Enough cat and mouse. "Lieutenant," I said, "is there something you want here?"

"Officially, no. Personally, I'm interested in what happens to Speer Galleries. How do you like your new position, Mr. Sommers?"

"I like it. Why?"

"Oh, I just thought one of the branch managers would end up as permanent director. Someone with administrative experience, you see. But of course the board had its reasons—I'm sure you're the best man for the job. Do you know what they were?"

I stared at him. "Do I know what *what* were?"

"What the board's reasons for selecting you were."

"I was informed only that I was the new director. The board didn't explain its reasoning processes to me."

"But surely you must have some idea?"

It was Lieutenant D'Elia who was saying it, but it was a Lieutenant Columbo trick, pure and simple. And Columbo's suspects all tripped themselves up by talking too much, by offering too much detail. "I don't know," I said.

"Now, Mr. Sommers, you're being modest—"

"I can tell you," Nedda interrupted. "The branch managers in London and Rome and Munich all hold their positions because of their knowledge of the European market. They're most valuable right where they are. The only branch manager we even considered was the man running the San Francisco gallery. But we decided he'd be Peter Principled beyond his capabilities if we put him in charge. Earl was the only logical choice."

"Process of elimination, I see," D'Elia nodded, meaning *So they worked they way down to you*. The board had appointed me director because Nedda had instructed them to. I got the feeling D'Elia knew that and wanted me to know he knew it. Then he fired a real bullet: "Did the board offer you the position before or after you and Mrs. Speer decided to marry?"

Mrs. Sommers, damn you. "I don't see that that's any of your business."

"As long as we have an unsolved murder on our books, Mr. Sommers, I can make it my business if I want to."

Nedda made a sound of contempt. "Meaning you can get away with murder, Lieutenant?"

"Well, I won't press the point—I can see it's a sore spot." My refusal to answer had been answer enough. "Tell me, Mr. Sommers, do you anticipate any special problems in running the galleries?"

"No. Why should I?"

"I was just wondering if it would be difficult to replace Mr. Wightman."

Nedda's head jerked up. "What's that? Replace Wightman?"

"No, it won't be any trouble at all," I said. "How did you know about that? It happened only this morning."

Nedda: "*What* happened only this morning?"

D'Elia answered her. "Mr. Wightman resigned."

She looked at me. "Earl?"

"That's right, he resigned. How did you find out so quickly, Lieutanent?"

D'Elia spread his hands. "Well now, Mr. Sommers, you can't expect me to disclose all my little secrets. Our sources of information are good only so long as we protect them. But Wightman's departure will leave a big hole, won't it?"

"Not for long. Quite a few porcelain experts are available."

"Glad to hear it. I hope you find a good one. Well, I've taken up enough of your time. Goodbye; Mrs. Sommers, and again, best wishes."

Nedda looked him straight in the eye and did not say thank you.

I showed the Lieutanent out and came back to face an angry-looking Nedda. "Earl, why did that man come here?"

I sank down into my leather chair. "I think," I said slowly, "I think he wanted me to know he's keeping an eye on me."

Her eyes narrowed. "You mean he thinks you had something to do with Amos's death?"

"Don't see how he could," I mused, thinking it was time to make this a team effort. "You and I both had alibis."

"Alibis! God, that's suspicious-sounding in itself."

"I didn't invent the word," I said irritably. "How did he find out so fast about Wightman? Somebody at the gallery must be reporting to him. A spy. A spy at Speer's. Terrific."

"Or else the place is bugged," Nedda said almost casually.

Bugged. I hadn't thought of that. That took the bloom off the rose, all right—the idea of that cop listening in to everything I said . . .

"Earl, did Wightman resign? Or did you fire him?"

"He resigned," I said, seeing a chance to spread a little butter. "I was planning to fire him, you know. But I decided you were right. He was too good an agent to let go just because he was a horse's ass."

"Why did he quit?"

"He decided to go into business for himself. He's setting up shop in San Francisco. Leonard Wightman is now a competitor."

Nedda was silent for a long time. Then: "Where'd he get the money?"

"What?"

"The money to start his own business. Where'd he get it? Amos once told me it was still possible to start on a shoestring when he opened his first gallery. But he said the nature of the business had changed so much in forty years that nobody could hope to make a go of it now without at least a year's operating expenses already in the bank before the doors ever opened. Now that's not something you just save up for, no matter how good your salary is. Somebody has to be bankrolling him."

Maybe not, I thought with a surge of excitement. I knew another way it could have been done.

The next day I called Triangle Inquiry Consultants and arranged to have my office checked for bugs. They came after hours that night and swept both my office and June Murray's, nothing.

I put June to work in the file room. Every negative report Wightman ever turned in, I told her, dating back to the day he first came to Speer's. I wanted the name and address of every owner of every piece of porcelain Wightman had turned down as unworthy of display at Speer Galleries. If I could do it with furniture, he could do it with porcelain.

The list June eventually compiled ran close to three hundred names. That's a lot of porcelain. I felt that same surge of excitement as when it first occurred to me Wightman might have been screwing Speer the same way I had been. I'd get the bastard yet. I called Triangle and asked for Valentine.

He caught on fast. "You suspect some irregularity," he said when I told him what I wanted him to do. "He reports the porcelain is worthless and then buys it for himself, is that it?"

"I think that's what's happened," I said.

"Have you confronted Mr. Wightman with your suspicions?"

"Wightman is no longer with us. He's gone into business for himself."

Again he caught on. "And that takes money. I see. Mr. Sommers, I'll need to know whether you intend to prosecute or not. Do I interview these people and find out what happened to their porcelain for your knowledge alone? Or do I go after evidence you can take to court?"

"Go after evidence," I said grimly. "I'm going to prosecute."

"Assuming Mr. Wightman is indeed guilty," Valentine said cautiously. "I'll be by this afternoon to pick up the list of names."

I hung up and leaned back in my William and Mary chair and allowed myself the luxury of an exultation that just might be premature. But I thought not. Sending Wightman to jail would be much more satisfying than firing him could ever have been. Good thing I hadn't given him the San Francisco branch—from the manager's office he'd have been able to rob us blind.

The phone buzzed. "Robin Coulter says the Queen Annes are here," June told me.

"Good girl," I said and dropped the receiver into the cradle. I hurried down to where the chairs were being unpacked. Robin had bought a perfect set of twelve—a real find. *If* they were as good as she said they were.

Robin was in the packing room, needlessly overseeing the two workmen doing the uncrating. She was excited and full of electricity, her bedroom eyes giving both workmen ideas they shouldn't be having. One of the chairs was already uncrated; I went over for a look.

Everybody likes Queen Anne style; it's graceful and easy to identify. This Philadelphia-made Queen Anne chair had been well cared for during the approximately two hundred fifty years of its life. What a beauty. The cabriole front legs, the S-curved back posts—everything molded into perfect unity of form. Those who laugh at the notion that furniture can be art should have seen that chair. And there were eleven more like it.

Robin was hunkered down, running a hand over one curved walnut front leg. "Isn't this a lovely patina, Earl?"

"It is indeed," I agreed enthusiastically. Everything about the chair was lovely. Queen Anne style takes its beauty from the fluidity of its line rather than from tacked-on ornamentation. Robin's chair had finely embroidered seat upholstery, but all the rest of the chair's appeal lay in its subtly controlled curves. Shortened arms, to allow for the voluminous dress of the day. Vase-shaped splat in a back slightly curved to fit the human body. But what really tickled my fancy about Queen Anne style was the crest rail—the top rail of the curved frame forming the back. The Queen Anne crest rail had a little dip in it, a smaller curve to fit the nape of the neck.

That little dip didn't last long in the American versions of Queen Anne—the fact that Robin's chair had it helped date the set from the first half of the eighteenth century. But in the English Queen Anne chairs that were the original models for their American cousins, the small scoop in the crest rail had had a very practical purpose behind it. The early 1700s were the time of those enormous, heavy, powdered wigs that added a couple of feet to a woman's height. The little dip in the top of the chair back was to allow the ladies to rest the weight of their wigs on the chair for a while. A chair designed to accommodate a hairstyle. Marvelous.

Robin had made a good buy. I toyed with the idea of postponing the display of the set so I could take one of the chairs home with me for a while. But Nedda had started making unfunny little jokes about our having to move out soon to make room for all the chairs.

"Congratulations, Robin," I told her. "You've pulled off something of a *coup*. We'll display them immediately."

"I know Sotheby's is interested," she said with a pleased smile.

"I'll bet they are," I laughed. "No, we'll deal with the museums on this one. I'll start the wheels rolling."

Then I gave her a congratulatory little hug, which she slipped out of a lot faster than she needed to.

Wightman's high-handed departure caused me trouble—just as he'd meant it to. It took me a full month to find a replacement and even then I'd had to settle for a second-stringer whose expertise was nothing to write home about. But I could always fire him as soon as I found someone better.

By the time I'd put my new porcelain "expert" to work, Valentine had a report for me.

"I'm sorry this is taking so long, Mr. Sommers," said the ever-courteous detective as he sat down across the cherry-wood table from me. "I've run into a number of snags. But you were right about Mr. Wightman. He was buying porcelain for himself."

"I knew it," I breathed.

"I'm only halfway through the list of names you gave me," Valentine said. "I've contacted a hundred forty of them. Of that number, thirty-seven said Mr. Wightman told them Speer's was not interested in what they had to sell and then called back a week later and offered to buy the porcelain himself. That was his pattern—first a no, then wait a week for them to feel the full weight of their disappointment, then a yes. The amounts he paid ranged from one hundred dollars to eight hundred dollars."

"Are these people willing to testify?"

"Direct testimony may not be necessary. Thirty of the thirty-seven have signed statements—they're in this folder."

"Why wouldn't the other seven sign?"

"General reluctance to sign anything of a legal nature—afraid they'd cause trouble for themselves. That's one of the snags I mentioned. The other is trying to trace people who've moved out of the Pittsburgh area. But thirty statements, Mr. Sommers—that's enough to go to court with. One or two examples of under-the-table deals can be explained away. But thirty—well, that establishes a pattern of intent to defraud. You'll want to consult your attorney, but I'm sure he'll tell you you have enough evidence to start legal proceedings. I don't think you'll need to contact the rest of the people on this list."

"All of them," I said stubbornly. "I want to know exactly how much that bastard cheated us out of."

Valentine gave me a look that said *It's your money* but answered, "Certainly, if you wish. Would you like weekly reports from now on?"

I told him that would be fine. When he'd left, I had June photocopy the thirty statements Valentine had brought in and deliver them to Peg McAllister.

It took Peg exactly ten minutes. She came bursting into my office, her eyes big and her mouth open. "What are you going to do, Earl?"

"Prosecute," I said calmly. "There'll be more evidence to come, but I want you to get started on it."

She sank down on a chair and moaned. "That's absolutely the *worst* thing you could do. You've been in this business long enough to know you don't advertise a thing like this. A dealer's livelihood depends upon his reputation. When one of your agents indulges in a little duplicity, you just get rid of him as quickly and quietly as possible."

"A little duplicity! That asshole has been stealing from us steadily for ten years. You want him to get away with it?"

"Earl, you're letting your dislike of the man override your better judgment. Stop and think. Once you bring this out in the open, everyone who's ever had any dealings with Wightman is going to start having second thoughts. We may be on the wrong end of a few lawsuits ourselves. You've already had this detective out talking to people—just asking questions is enough to start them wondering. What do you suppose they're thinking about now? They're thinking about how much they can gouge out of Speer Galleries, that's what they're thinking about."

"We're not liable for what Wightman did on his own."

"The hell we aren't. We sent him—he was accepted by those people as our agent, acting for us. *We* can prosecute Wightman if we want to, but the people he cheated can sue the pants off us."

Damn. This wasn't going to be as tidy as I thought. "All right, make a legal-type suggestion."

"Get hold of Wightman. Tell him what you've got on him. Offer to buy the porcelain for exactly what he paid for it. Then make reparation to the people he cheated and go on and sell the stuff for what it's really worth."

"Oh, hell, Peg, you don't think he still has the porcelain, do you? Where do you think he got the money to go into business for himself?"

She nodded, accepting it. "Then give him the chance to make reparation himself. Anything to keep Speer's name clean. And call off that damned detective!"

Peg kept on in the same vein for another ten or fifteen minutes. Finally I told her I'd have to think about it and shooed her out. Damn. Damn, damn, *damn!* This wasn't going the way I wanted at all. I finally had the goods on that horsefaced Englishman and I couldn't do a blooming thing about it. If we could intimidate him into paying a fair price for the porcelain he'd finagled—well, that might do it. He'd go backrupt trying to come up with all that money at once. But what did we have to threaten him with? Wightman might be willing to gamble that we'd never risk prosecuting him.

Buzz, buzz. "A Mr. Bates on line one," June said.

"Who?"

"Charles Bates. He says he's an old buddy of yours."

Charlie Bates. I tried to swallow, but my throat was dry.

"Are you there?" June asked.

"I'll take it." I pressed the button numbered one. "Charlie?"

"Hey, Earl, old buddy!" came that nauseatingly familiar voice. "Long time no see! Hey, you really hit it big, didn't you, buddy?"

My breath was short. "How are you, Charlie?"

"Couldn't be better." He laughed. "Bet you never thought you'd hear that!"

"I've been wondering where you were, Charlie."

An even bigger laugh. "Yeah, I bet! Hey, buddy, I wanna talk to you. Can you get away?"

"Now?"

"No time like the present."

"Well, I have an appointment—"

"Cancel it. Meet me in an hour. By the yaks."

"Where?"

"By the yaks, the yaks. You know—the yaks in the zoo? Where we met that other time? Remember?"

He said *that other time* with such an insidious snicker that my stomach turned over. "I remember."

"Great. One hour. See ya, buddy."

"See ya," I echoed absently, and sat there for a full minute with a dead phone in my hand.

8

Traffic was nasty; I had to give my full attention to staying alive. When the moon is full, every other driver in Pittsburgh breaks out with some kind of death wish. At such times you find yourself saying little prayers as you grip the wheel. I finally pulled into one of the Highland Park lots and walked toward the yak pens. Charlie wasn't there yet; I was early.

I sat down on a bench and glared at two surly-looking beasts who glared right back. Charlie's call hadn't been a total surprise, of course; I'd been halfway expecting it. What I didn't know was how much Charlie would try to bleed me for. The yak pens made a good place to meet: just isolated enough that blackmailer and victim could talk with little danger of being overheard. A new position for me—I'd never let myself be manuvered into a spot like this one before. In spite of the lump in my chest, I was curious to see how Charlie planned on handling it. Even he had to see there was no way of exposing me without incriminating himself.

Or maybe he didn't; maybe he thought he'd found a way. Charlie had never won any prize for smarts. He'd probably worked out some cockamamie scheme with enough holes in it to send us both up. The problem was, I didn't feel confident I could talk him around this time. This time, I'd be talking to a murderer. A man who had killed another man was not subject to usual methods of control. As long as we'd known each other I'd been able to manipulate him, so now I was having trouble adjusting to this new reality: I was actually afraid of Charlie.

The weather was beginning to cool a little. Only a few other zoo visitors passed my bench, most of them looking as if they wished they were somewhere else. One man was noticeable for the contrast he offered as he strode along the asphalt walk with a gaudily wrapped package crooked in one arm. One of those cock-of-the-walk types—the kind that expects lesser folk to get out of the way. I was shocked all the way down to my toes when I realized it was Charlie Bates I was watching.

Something had changed. Gone was that hangdog look that had been Charlie's trademark all his life. His clothes were good—and they fit. There was a bounce in his step I'd never seen before. Yes, something had definitely changed.

"Gladaseeya, gladaseeya, gladaseeya!" he started booming at me while he was still seventy-five feet away. Charlie the whiner—*booming* at me?

I said something and he said something and he sat down, putting the gaudy package on the bench beside him. He lowered his voice to a normal conversational level and said, "Man, is it good to see you! I dint want to call too soon—after the wedding, y'know. How long's it been?"

"Almost four months."

"Four months! My best buddy Earl's been married four months! And I thought you'd never take the plunge. Y'know, sometimes I used to worry about you, Earl. 'Bout you never getting married, I mean. Sometimes it makes a guy wonder, y'know."

I stared at him, astonished.

"Oh, I dint really think that," he said in a rush, not wanting to hurt my feelings. "And I'm glad you went ahead and done it. But you sure surprised me, marrying the old man's widow like that. You can be a close-mouthed sonuvagun when you want to, Earl. Haw! You got yourself a real dish there. Not to mention *all that money*." He opened his big mouth all the way and laughed and laughed.

I decided my best bet was to try to match his mood. "Say, buddy, tell me why I had to break an appointment. Why'd you drag me out here to smell the yaks?"

He looked surprised. "I don't think they smell so bad." He turned to watch four or five of the huge animals gently bumping shoulders. "'Smatter of fact," he said softly, "I think they're kinda grand." He turned back to me. "You want to know why I gotcha out here. All right. I gotcha out here to thank you, Earl. You saved my life, old buddy." He laughed at the expression on my face. "You don't know what the hell I'm talking about, do you? Well, I'll tell you. Earl, dint you ever wonder what happened that day—at Speer's house?"

Didn't I ever wonder. I said dryly, "Yes, Charlie. I wondered."

"Well, I'll tell you what happened. I was reborn."

Reborn. Why did I have the feeling I was being set up for a punch line? "You mean you got religion?"

Charlie laughed so loudly that one of the yaks ambled over to the edge of the pen to see what all the fuss was about. "You could say that," Charlie grinned at me. "You could say I got a kind of religion. What I got, Earl, was a purpose in life. And you made it happen. Listen. You ever pointed a loaded gun at a man, Earl? Course not. You don't know what it's like—holding the power of life and death in your hand. And then having the guts to *use* that power."

"Charlie," I said firmly, "tell me exactly what happened."

"Well, Speer was out back in the garden, like you said. Just sitting there, tired of digging, I guess. Sitting there like God Almighty looking out over what he'd created. I got up real close to him before he saw me. Then he just looked up sort of casual-like and saw this gun pointing in his face. Y'know what happened? Earl, it was like watching God Almighty fall on his face. That old guy was terrified. He turned white and his mouth was working and his hands was shaking and he just kept staring up the barrel of the gun. He was scared to death. He was scared of *me*."

"So what happened?"

"He thought I was a burglar, see, and when he could talk he started babbling about how he'd open his safe for me if I'd just leave his porcelain alone. He was shaking he was so scared, but I was starting to feel pretty good. He was too old to fight back, and I wasn't in no hurry. So I just took my good old time. I told him I wasn't there to rob him. I told him I was there to kill him, and you'd sent me."

"You *what?!*"

Charlie waved a hand in the air. "Nothing to worry about. No way that shaking old man was gonna get the jump on me—Earl, you'da had to see him to understand. He wasn't gonna challenge me. I had the gun. And I thought you'd like him to know before he went. Know that you'd won, I mean. Think about it, Earl. Think about him knowing."

I thought about it. I thought about Amos Speer spending the last moments of his life understanding that he'd made a fatal mistake, that he'd taken on the wrong man when he went after me. Understanding that it was Earl Sommers who was running the show now. In spite of the risk Charlie had taken, I found myself beginning to smile.

Charlie laughed. "Thought you'd like that. You know what he did when I told him? Earl, it was the weirdest thing I ever seen. He just gave up. He gave up right then. This rich, important sonuvabitch just kinda melted down to nothing when I pointed the gun at him and told him he was gonna die. He wasn't even scared no more—he was just beaten. He just turned into a blob of jelly. He wasn't gonna fight back, he wasn't gonna do nothing." Charlie made a face of distaste. "He was disgusting."

The thought crossed my mind that Charlie had at last got a glimpse of the picture he himself had always presented to the world.

"It was the gun, y'know," Charlie was saying. "It was all because of the gun. If I'da went there without no weapon, he wouldn'ta just give up like that. Like the gun was some kinda magic wand. All I had to do was wave it around a little and everthing changed. All my life I let other people beat me down. All my life. But now I had a gun in my hand, and this big shot who wouldn't even see me if he passed me on the street—well, he just give in to me. To me. Charlie Bates."

I didn't say anything as I let what he was saying sink in. Charlie was making a cooing noise at the yak standing at the edge of the pen. "Then what?" I asked. "Then did you shoot him?"

"Not yet. I told him if he wanted to live a little longer, he could show me around the house. I always wanted to see how guys like him lived." Enjoying his power over Amos Speer, stretching it out, making it last. "Man, that place is a *castle!* And my old buddy Earl's living in it now! We went all over the place, he showed me everthing. He done whatever I told him. Then I got hungry and told him to fix me something to eat. We went into the kitchen and he fixed me a salad. A salad, haw! He had this sharp knife in his hand and I kept hoping he'd try something, but he didn't."

I rather liked the picture of the great Amos Speer chopping onions for Charlie Bates. A guided tour and lunch—that would account for the gap between the time I saw Charlie into a cab and the time Speer died. And it explained why the body was found in the house instead of the garden. "You took him back into the living room to shoot him," I prompted.

Charlie nodded. "Y'know, Earl, it was kinda weird. All the time we were looking at the house, the time we spent in the kitchen—I felt like I really knew the guy. Y'understand? Never saw him before in my life, but I felt I known him a long time. Everything about him was familiar—the wavy hair, the size of his hands. I could draw you a picture right now of how his fingernails was shaped. I got kinda fond of the old guy. The way you feel about a sick old dog you gotta put out of its misery. So I wasn't mean to him, Earl. I just took him into the living room and told him to turn sideways so I could shoot him in the temple. And he did it! No argument, no fighting back."

"Why the temple?"

"No reason. I just felt like it. So then I shot him, Earl. One shot, just like you said. He was dead before he hit the floor. He was dead, and I was alive—more alive than I ever been! I went there wanting to die, and I ended up getting excited about being alive!" He dropped his voice to a conspiratorial level. "Earl, I got a hard-on. I ain't gonna tell you how long it was since the last time. It made me feel good to kill that old man, Earl, doncha see? *It made me feel good*."

I saw. Good lord yes, I saw. I saw and I wished I didn't.

"So, I skedaddled outa there," Charlie went on. "I took some money from the old guy's billfold—not all of it, just enough to carry me for a while. Guess the police saw what was left and figured he hadn't been robbed at all. I sat around a coupla weeks, waiting to see if the cops could trace the shooting to me. They couldn't. Y'know Leyton Samuels?"

"What?"

"Leyton Samuels. Y'know the name?"

The abrupt change of subject threw me a little. "Uh, Samuels—let me see. Labor man, something to do with unions. Wasn't he the one who was killed a couple of months ago?"

"That's the one."

"What about him?"

"Me."

"You? You what?"

"I did that."

I could barely speak. "You? *You* did that?"

"Yep. And that rich old woman in Squirrel Hill—hear about her?"

"Charlie—"

"And Frank Hellinger, the newspaper guy?"

"You killed all those people? *You?* In god's name why, Charlie?"

Charlie was enjoying himself. "The pay was right. You'd be surprised how many people are willing to pay to get other people put out of the way. I told ya I have a purpose in life now, Earl. I've turned pro."

Charlie broke off as a woman and a small girl approached, the daughter dragging her feet and the mother trying to keep her temper. When they'd passed Charlie went on, "I finally found something I can do and I like doing. That's never happened before, Earl. Y'understand what that means to me? I'm still new at the game, but already I'm making more money'n I ever made before in my life."

I was floundering. "Well, that's, uh."

"You know what I did, Earl? I just left everything. Everthing! Apartment, clothes, even the people I knew—I just walked away from 'em all. I got a new life now. I'm living good, I don't owe nobody—Earl, you remember the mob was after me?"

"Uh, yeah."

"Well, they're paying *me* now!" Charlie was riding high all right. "I cleared up my debt and let 'em know I was available. Those fellas have turned out to be good customers."

"That's. Terrific."

"And Earl, I got me a woman you wouldn't believe. Everthing's breaking right for me—"

"Charlie, why are you telling me all this?"

"Oh, you'll never talk," he said blandly. "You got as much to lose as me. But I figured I owed you an explanation. After all, if it wasn't for you I'da never found my true calling."

What do you say to a man who tells you he's at last found his calling in life, and that "calling" is killing people? What I said was "Congratulations!"—and I said it as many ways as I could think of. Charlie the loser, irrationally transformed into a professional killer! Charlie Bates—*a hit man*.

Bigmouth Charlie was still talking. "Thass why I wanted to see you. To thank you. You made it happen. You saved my life, Earl. So I owe you, old buddy."

"Ah, that's all right, Charlie, you don't owe me anything—"

"But I do. Is there something I can do for you? Some little favor—"

"No, no!" I said, alarmed.

"All right, but I'll find some way to pay you back." I didn't like the sound of that very much. "Y'know, before I left Speer's house, I took something for you." He picked up the gaudy package; I'd forgotten about it. "It's one of them little statues he had in cases all over the place, uh, the porcelain things. I knew you liked stuff like that." He laughed. "Course, I didn't know then you were gonna end up with it all. Anyhow, here it is. Like a souvenir."

A souvenir. Souvenir of a murder. "Charlie, you are truly incredible," I said sincerely as I took the package.

"Aw, thass all right," he said deprecatingly. "Just a little something to remember me by."

Oh, I'll remember you, all right. We sat without talking for a minute or two as Charlie watched the yak, and that alone told me how much he'd changed. Charlie had always been an overemotional, nonstop talker, afraid of silences. He was still garrulous, but his talk now was that of a man who was sure of his audience. He was the one who'd directed our conversation, not me. He'd even had enough self-assurance to tell me to think something over and then wait while I did.

Suddenly Charlie hopped up with that newfound energy of his. He stuck out his hand. "Goodbye, old buddy. And good luck."

I shook his hand, remembering the last time we'd gone through the ritual. "Goodbye, Charlie. Stay healthy."

"Count on it." He turned and walked away with the jaunty air of a man who knows he's got the world on a string.

He lifted a hand without turning his head—a farewell salute. I hoped to god that was the last time I'd ever see my old buddy Charlie Bates.

The yak was staring at me with a baleful eye. Suddenly I was cold—cold right down to my bones. I hurried to the parking lot and drove back to the gallery in a daze, miraculously escaping getting killed on the way.

June Murray looked up from her desk as I passed through, saw the gaud package under my arm, and said brightly, "Somebody give you a present?"

"No calls, June." I closed the door and put the package on the cherrywood table. Then I sat down and dropped my head into my hands.

Charlie Bates a hit man! Contract killers were tall men who wore black suits and tinted glasses and never spoke much. They were cool and smart and taciturn—the exact opposite of Charlie Bates. This must be the most fantastic piece of miscasting since Richard Nixon was elected President. How had he managed it? How had Charlie Bates suddenly stood up and taken control of his life? And what a way to take control!

All the old clichés about sex and violence came rushing to mind. Charlie had had two loaded guns, one in his hand and one in his pants. Spurting out life and death, feeling like God. Just one more nothing little man who'd found his courage in a gun. And even that consolation he hadn't discovered for himself; on his own Charlie had given up, he'd been ready to die. He could have gone to his grave without ever knowing about the kicks and the money and the feeling of omnipotence a gun could give him.

And I'd been the one who put the gun in his hand.

In a way, Charlie had gone through with his self-destructive intentions after all. It had been a symbolic suicide; he'd had to kill off the old Charlie Bates before the new one could come into being. *I was reborn,* he'd said, thinking he was making a joke. But that was exactly what had happened—he'd been born again with a vigor the God-exploiters themselves would have envied. And that made me a kind of midwife, I guess. It was a totally different Charlie I'd helped bring into the world—a man who acted instead of one who sat back waiting for things to happen to him.

The people he'd killed, the people he was yet to kill—I couldn't let myself think about them. And what if Charlie's new profession suddenly turned sour on him for some reason? Would he blame me for that, the way he'd credited me with steering him in the right direction in the first place? I couldn't think about that either.

Charlie had taken charge; sick as it sounded, he had stature now. It wasn't that he'd suddenly grown a new set of brains. He still saw nothing, he still understood nothing—he was the same woeful ignoramus he'd always been. He was still dumb enough to think I'd done him a favor when I sent him out to do my dirty work for me. The twist the murder had taken was something I could never have anticipated. But Charlie's peabrain still thought in simplistic equations: Earl Sommers plus gun equals the good life for Charlie Bates. I was the accidental beneficiary of Charlie's "rebirth," and I should have been relieved it had worked out that way. So why was I sitting there sweating?

It was Charlie's new self-confidence that was scaring me. No, it was more than just confidence: he was aggressive now, even arrogant, even in little things. *Cancel it*, he'd told me when I said I had an appointment. A man is still judged by the visual image he projects, and it may have been that arrogant quality that enabled him to come to terms with the mob. Ignorance and arrogance, the most dangerous combination there is.

I sat staring at the gaudy package in front of me on the table. Incriminating evidence Lieutenant D'Elia would give his eyeteeth to get hold of. I reached for the package; might as well see what Charlie Bates considered an appropriate souvenir of murder.

It was the Meissen Leda. Brown eyes and all.

9

Thus began the winter of my discontent, said Shakespeare or Emily Dickinson or Art Buchwald. I didn't hear from Charlie again; he disappeared into that new world of money and murder he'd found for himself. But other things—my god, the other things.

First, Robin Coulter. Eventually she'd come around, but for the moment I wasn't getting anywhere. Before Amos Speer died, she'd been full of animosity—prickling at everything I said, looking for excuses to insult me. But once I became The Boss, she'd had to pull back, watch what she said. She even had to work at being friendly. I got a lot of laughs out of that. Oh yeah, I laughed *good*. I even encouraged her in her hesitant attempts at camaraderie. Every chance I got, I encouraged her. Once I had her in a horizontal position she wouldn't be so high and mighty.

But she was proving a hard case. In December one day I gave her bottom a friendly little squeeze. She whirled on me and said she couldn't think of a single reason why she should go on working for a man who thought he had the right to put his hands on her whenever he felt like it. Jeez. So I sent her off to Europe on a buying trip; it was the wrong time of year, but a bribe was clearly in order.

Next, Peg McAllister kept hammering at me that not only were we liable to the people Wightman had cheated, we'd better get a move on and settle up fast. She said the best thing to do would be pay off all those people quietly. "Then we can put the word out in the business, Earl, without going to court, without headlines. Let the other dealers know how much Wightman cost us. That'll cook his goose in the long run. Nobody'll deal with him because nobody'll trust him. And the customers will eventually catch on there's something not quite kosher about Leonard Wightman's gallery in San Francisco."

Wightman had opened to a roll of drums and a blare of trumpets, California style. Right away he'd cut into the profits of our west coast branch, but part of it might be a novelty appeal that would wear off in time. But I sure as hell couldn't count on it. And it galled me to think I'd end up paying off Wightman's victims to protect the professional reputation of Speer Galleries. "Peg, I'm not convinced we ought to pay up meekly and hope some higher justice will catch up with Wightman in the future. Besides, we don't know the real value of that porcelain—why, it could cost us a fortune." A wild guess: it might run to half a million. I didn't know. And I didn't want to find out.

"All right," Peg said, "if you're determined to prosecute. But do it this way—pay off the people Wightman cheated *first*. Admit liability publicly. *Then* take the bastard to court. The courts will force him to repay whatever we paid out, and that'll put him out of business in a hurry. It might even have some favorable publicity value—show the world how honest and conscientious Speer's is. But no prosecution without first making things right with the folks Wightman rooked. Absolutely not. It would be suicidal."

Which meant I'd still have to pay out the money and then gamble the courts would see things our way. "How certain are you we'd get a favorable judgment?"

Lawyer-like, she hedged. "Nothing's certain in any judicial process. I feel confident we'd win. I have to admit your detective—Valentine, is that his name?—he did a good job. We have the evidence. But it's time that's important, Earl. We have to negotiate with the victims and reach an equitable settlement, and that's going to take a while. You know damn well some of them are going to hire themselves smart lawyers and then the price will go up and up and up. They've got us over a barrel—we'll just have to pay. But Earl, we have a good chance of getting it all back. Better than good—excellent."

An excellent chance. But still a chance, not a certainty. "Damn it, Peg, I don't like getting stuck with Wightman's bill. Even if we do get it back later, and we're not even sure of that."

"Then the only alternative is to get Wightman to pay up himself."

"And how do we do that? Give me a weapon, Peg, something I can beat him over the head with."

"Just tell him what we're going to do. Give him a deadline. Tell him if full reparation isn't made by such and such a date, *we'll* step in and pay the bill. And then we'll take him for every cent he's got."

"You think that'll do it?"

"It might."

It might. Yes indeedy it just might. And if threats failed to make him assume the responsibility, we could still fall back on the lawsuit. "Okay, I'll give it a shot. Wightman might think we're bluffing, though—he doesn't think the way normal people do. I'll go show him our evidence. But in case he won't admit culpability, why don't you start drawing up some sort of legal form we can get his victims to sign? Something that says they have accepted fair and honest recompense from us, that Speer's is no longer liable, blah blah. You know what I mean."

"I've already done that," she sniffed.

I decided to put off my flying trip to San Francisco until January in spite of Peg's urging haste. I didn't want to abandon Nedda during the holidays. In fact I stuck to her like a leech, because—surprise, surprise—I had a little problem there. Nedda had taken a lover.

I hadn't confronted her about it; I wasn't ready for a showdown. I didn't know who he was or where they met for their illicit assignations or any of the other lurid details. I just knew he existed. Nedda no longer came prowling after me in that pantherlike way of hers; she *allowed* me to make love to her, the way a cat allows itself to be stroked. And she enjoyed it about the same way, as homage due her. But on nights I came home too tired to perform, she just rolled over carelessly and went to sleep. She didn't need me. She was getting it somewhere else.

So I made sure she didn't spend even one hour of the holidays with him, whoever he was. And in the meantime I looked at her check stubs. No large amounts made out to cash, at least. That was one indulgence I refused to tolerate. Nedda had spent plenty on me when she was still married to Speer.

Nedda was a beautiful woman. Not a very nice woman, but a beautiful one. And sexy as hell. She no more had to pay a lover than Cleopatra. She'd given me expensive gifts and even handed me cash on occasion because it amused her to do so. It was her none too subtle way of reminding me which of us held the upper hand. I'd let her get away with it; sure, why not? It had paid off. But Nedda liked playing games, and she'd just started a new one with a new player. I didn't know anything about this guy, and rule one was always know your enemy.

So I made one more call to Valentine.

San Francisco in January is nothing like the travel posters say. It's damp and chill, with that watery sun everywhere, smilin' through. At least on the east coast all that rotten weather tells you exactly what time of year it is.

A discreet plaque on the door said *Wightman Porcelains*. Not as much floorspace as our branch, but the pieces Wightman was displaying were good. He must have been planning this for years. I told his receptionist—Miss Centerfold of All Times—who I was and that I wanted to see her boss. I rested my attaché case on her desk while she used the phone.

"Ah, there you are, dear boy," came the familiar whinny. "I just knew you wouldn't be able to keep yourself away—scouting out the competition, is that it? Do look around. Try not to turn too green."

He'd come from somewhere in the back of the gallery; I gestured in that direction. "Is your office back there?"

"Yes, it is," he said—pointedly not inviting me in.

"We need to talk, Wightman. Let's go to your office."

"Dear me, I see you haven't learned a thing, Sommers. You don't invite yourself into someone else's office. You wait to *be* invited." He said all this with such a rolling of the eyes and a twitching of the eyebrows that Miss Centerfold giggled.

I remembered all the times he'd pushed his way into my office but didn't remind him; it was exactly the kind of quibble Wightman loved. "We need to talk," I repeated. "Now."

I must have said it right because he abandoned his opening gambit. "Oh, very well," he said petulantly. "Don't have a temper tantrum. If it's talk that makes you happy, by all means let us talk." He turned and strode toward the back, leaving me to trail after him.

He closed the office door behind me and flapped a hand toward one wall. "I've been offered a hundred and fifty thousand for that. But of course it'll go for much more."

He was referring to a shell-carved kneehole block-front desk against the wall. Good Newport workmanship, Townsend-Goddard school. Wightman was probably right; he'd be able to get more than a hundred fifty thousand for it. Those pieces always sold for more than they were worth. But the kneehole desk was strictly for show, to impress visitors. Wightman's working desk was a Walter Gropius design. It figured.

"You're dealing furniture too?" I asked. "The plaque out front says porcelains."

"Just a sideline—nothing serious. It offers me a kind of rough-hewn relaxation, don't you know. Porcelain can be so demanding, I need a change of pace once in a while. You probably work out in a gym."

Wightman must be losing his touch; I wasn't even tempted. I sat down without waiting for an invitation and opened the attaché case. I took out copies of the statements signed by the people Wightman had bilked and dropped them on his desk. "Better take a look."

Wightman arched an eyebrow at me. "*Better* take a look?" he repeated. "Or what? Do you have some menacing threat to back that up?"

"Look, you horse's ass, I'm doing you a favor by coming here. You're in trouble, Wightman, and I can't say I'm sorry. How much trouble depends on what you do now. Look at the papers."

"Dear me, that *is* menacing. I am all a-tremble." With one finger he casually flipped open the folder holding the statements. He glanced at the first one, turned it over, glanced at the second. When he'd looked at no more than four or five, he closed the folder. "Yes?"

"Yes? What do you mean, *yes?* Do you understand what those are?"

He chuckled. "Of course I understand, dear boy. Don't assume everyone has the same sluggish mental processes you do."

I stared at him. I'd just shown him I had evidence he was a thief, and he was acting as unconcerned as if I'd said it was going to rain. "Then you understand we're in a position to prosecute? You don't think we're just going to let this pass, do you? If you don't make reparation to those people you ripped off, then we will. And if *we* have to pay for your sticky fingers, then you can be damned sure *you'll* pay. And pay and pay and pay. You'll lose your pretty new gallery, do you understand that?"

Wightman was looking at me as if I were some interesting new specimen. "Feeling your power, old chap? Give a nonentity a little authority and look what happens! Your assumption of godhood doesn't suit you, dear boy. You don't have the style for it."

"A delaying tactic, Wightman? It won't work. One way or another, those people are going to be repaid. The only question to be decided is whether you go to jail or not."

Wightman threw back his head and brayed. "Oh, you are a jewel, Sommers! True to form in every way—predictable as a bowel movement. Now if you can bring yourself to concentrate for a full thirty seconds, I'll try to explain a few things in words of one syllable or less. In the first place, you're not going to involve the grand old name of Speer Galleries in a scandalous lawsuit. Dear me, no. Even if you did win, the name of Speer would be suspect for years among the overendowed upper classes of this country that form the backbone of our business. In the second place, you'd have to prove I resold that porcelain for personal profit at the expense of Speer's good name. Now do you really think you have the acumen to trace all that porcelain?"

There I thought I had him. "I don't have to. All we have to prove is one or two cases, and we have a lot to work from." I wasn't sure about that, but it seemed a safe gamble. "Are you willing to risk losing your gallery on the assumption we won't be able to trace even *one* sale?"

Wightman pursed his lips in a mock pout. "Alas, no, I confess I'm not. All this is *très fade*, Sommers—but if you insist on playing your little game out to its sordid end, so be it." He got up from his desk and walked unhurriedly over to a wall safe. From the safe he took a large envelope which he casually tossed in my direction; I had to make a fumbling catch to keep from being hit in the face. "Now *you* had better take a look," he said, sitting back down. "Turnabout and all that."

What was he up to? I opened the envelope and began to read the papers.

They were all signed statements from the people *I* had bilked—the ones who'd sold me valuable pieces of furniture cheaply, pieces I'd resold for personal profit.

Wightman was grinning wickedly. "You're not the only one who can hire a detective."

He had me. God damn his smirking, conniving hide—he had me good. I'd never take legal action against him, I'd even end up paying off his victims. And he knew it. The bastard really had me.

"You went about it in a remarkably unintelligent way, Sommers, even for you." He was really enjoying himself. "Selling most of the pieces to Speer's under assumed names. Well, really. A more inept piece of subterfuge I've never come across. My detective found it embarrassingly easy to uncover your trail. So you see, dear boy, I have more on you than you'll ever have on me. You're not exactly in a position to make threats, are you?"

Jesus Christ. God damn it to hell. "So now what?"

"I won't use the term gentlemen's agreement," Wightman said, "because you'd never understand the meaning of the word. But I do like to think of myself as a reasonable man, willing to make concessions in the service of professional harmony."

"Mutual blackmail," I said bluntly.

He smiled with an aggravating blandness. "I have no objection to the term. Mutual blackmail it shall be. We both just forget this unpleasant little interlude in our lives and go our separate ways—which, I predict, will be to the top of the heap for me and the slough of despond for you. Poetic justice, I do love it so. I might point out that those statements you are grasping so fervidly in your sweaty hand are simply one of five sets. The originals and three sets of copies are in other hands, safe from any blundering derring-do you might be contemplating."

"Wightman, I'll get you yet," I said, sounding melodramatic even to my own ears.

Wightman blinked his eyes and then opened a drawer of his desk. He took out a small piece of paper which he silently handed me. On the paper he'd written: "I'll get you somehow, Wightman." He took the statements from me and put them back in his safe. "As I say, Sommers, you are depressingly predictable. I can even tell you what you'll do when you get back to Pittsburgh. But I won't—life should hold some surprises, even for the likes of you." He came back to the deak, put the folder I'd brought back into my attaché case, closed the case, pointedly handed it to me. "Now run along like a good boy and play your clumsy little games elsewhere. Try not to disturb the grown-ups. Go, Sommers. Go now."

I banged the attaché case down on its studs and drew it hard across the surface of the Walter Gropius desk. It left four deep scratches.

"Get out!" Wightman was screeching as I left. "Get out, you aborigine!"

As I passed the reception desk, Miss Centerfold looked up. "Come back soon," she smiled.

I remembered the last time I'd sat on a plane and tried to figure out a way to save my neck. That time it had been Charlie Bates, and I'd ended up deciding to kill him. It didn't work out that way, but the fact that I'd been able to make such a decision must mean something. Desperate situations, etc. And god knows things were desperate now.

Someday, somehow, I'd get that bastard Englishman; I swore it. But Wightman would have to wait; there were more urgent matters. Money, for one. Somewhere I was going to have to find the funds to pay off those fools who'd sold their porcelain so cheaply. I couldn't just let the whole thing drop—I'd sent Valentine to talk to them, I'd brought Peg McAllister in on it. I'd let it go too far.

Something Peg had said was bothering me. She'd claimed that the very act of asking questions would make Wightman's victims suspect something was fishy about the deals they'd made with him. If that were true about my detective and Wightman's victims, wouldn't it be equally true about Wightman's detective and the suckers *I'd* taken? Were there people out there right now thinking about making trouble for me?

The only way I could be sure I was safe was to see that those people were adequately reimbursed as well. Where in the name of heaven was the money coming from?

Horrible first thought: Sell the Duprée chair.

No. It might not be enough, for one thing. And there had to be some other way—funnel the profits from the European branches into a special fund, then think up some explanation that would satisfy Peg. Or at least keep her quiet. Because of Peg, I'd have to take care of Wightman's victims first. That meant I'd be covering up his double-dealing while my own peccadillos went unprotected. I would get him for this, yes I would, someday I would really get him.

That whole business of Wightman's having me investigated was curious. What had put him on to it? He himself had been asking for an investigation when he suddenly showed up with enough money to open his own gallery. But I'd done nothing like that. I'd simply married my money; happens all the time. But something must have started him looking.

I closed my eyes and tried to remember what I could of the statements he'd shown me. At least two of them were dated December, just last month. Wightman's investigation had been recent, then—just completed, in fact. So he probably didn't start looking until a short time ago. Not until I was investigating him.

Not until I was investigating him. I remembered the casual way he'd taken the news that I had evidence of his chicanery, almost as if he'd been expecting it. No almost: he *had* been expecting it. He had known what I was doing, and he'd taken steps to protect himself. He wouldn't have gone looking for evidence incriminating me if he hadn't known he would need it. Someone had tipped him off.

Lieutenant D'Elia had known of Wightman's resignation the same day it happened. Since then I'd more or less dismissed the idea of a spy reporting to outsiders as too preposterous to be taken seriously. Spies within the business, yes—but an eclectic snitch? Sounded nutty, but that must be it. Somebody at Speer's was moonlighting as a pipeline-for-hire.

Who knew about my investigation of Wightman? I dismissed Nedda; she knew something was in the wind but I'd told her no details. That left only three people: Peg McAllister, June Murray, and me. I knew I hadn't tipped Wightman off, even accidentally. And Peg McAllister would shoot herself before she'd do anything to harm the business.

That left June.

It made sense. When I'd first started my investigation of Wightman's private deals, I'd sent June to the file room to dig out all the negative reports he'd ever filed, as a starting point for Valentine. In order to conduct a similar investigation of me, Wightman would've had to have access to the negative reports *I* had filed. June already knew how to go about looking for damaging evidence. She was the logical one to supply Wightman with the ammunition he'd needed.

I spent the rest of the flight back to Pittsburgh working on a plan for dealing with my oh-so-perfect secretary.

10

The first thing I noticed when I got home from San Francisco was a nick in the leg of a maple Pilgrim chair I'd bought only the week before.

"How did it happen?" I demanded of Nedda. "How could you possibly have let it happen?"

She raised a lazy eyebrow at me. "I'm supposed to stand guard over your chairs? The cleaning service was here yesterday. It must have happened then."

I was appalled. "The cleaning service? You let the cleaning service handle my chairs?"

Nedda looked amused. "What are they supposed to do—skip every room that has one of your chairs in it? They'd end up cleaning just the kitchen and the bathrooms."

"And I suppose they sit on them and rest in between chores," I said in disgust.

"They know better than that. This service is used to handling antiques—normally they're very careful. Earl, if you insist on keeping those chairs here instead of in the gallery where they belong, you shouldn't be too surprised when an accident happens."

"Get a new cleaning service. A bonded one. I can't have this kind of thing. I don't know if that nick can be—"

"They're all bonded," Nedda said with an edge in her voice. "And what makes you think the next service would be better? It'd probably be worse. The service we use is a good one, and I'm not going to all the trouble of looking for a better one just because you've cluttered up the house with more antique chairs than anyone could possibly want."

"I want them," I pointed out. "And I want them here. Nedda, if you'd ever take the time to look at the chairs—really look at them—you wouldn't see them as clutter."

"Every time I turn around I stumble over one of those damned chairs," she snapped. "Amos's porcelain, at least, doesn't take up much room. You men and your little acquisitions."

"You don't exactly live the spartan life yourself," I said mildly. "Come on, Nedda, it's not worth quarreling about."

"Not so long as you get your way. Earl, I don't mind a few goodies stolen from the gallery, but you've gone too far. Who was it said moderation in all things?"

"Columbia Pictures," I said promptly, trying for a light note. "Some guy talking to Ronald Colman in *Lost Horizon*."

She didn't smile.

Time for the branches' quarterly reports, and I got a shock: Speer Galleries' overall profits were down. I'd expected it of the San Francisco office—Wightman's doing. And I'd put a lot of the home office money into my chair collection—all recoverable, of course. But it was the London branch that was the surprise; it showed a dip in profits that was totally unexpected. And the fault, I was angry to learn, lay in the new rare books department.

I read through the report submitted by the woman I'd put in charge. Her name was Deborah Ainsley and she'd written a wordy account of how rare books moved in long-term cycles and how we were now in the buying half of the cycle. Two years from now, she promised, the investments she was making now would pay off handsomely.

Maybe. I got on the phone and called H. L. Sprogg, the London branch manager. I asked him about the Ainsley woman's explanation of long-term cycles in the rare books trade. "Straight answer, Mr. Sprogg. Do rare books move in cycles?"

He hesitated. Then: "I don't really know, Mr. Sommers. Rare books—well, they don't seem to follow any normal rules that I can see. Also, they require a very, very specialized kind of knowledge." He hesitated again. "That's why I was so concerned when you appointed Mrs. Ainsley to establish a rare books department."

I remembered he'd harrumphed a little but he hadn't really said anything. "If you didn't think she was qualified, you should have told me so at the time."

Again that hesitation. "If you'll remember, Mr. Sommers, you presented me with a *fait accompli.* You did not consult me, you informed me. I thought it extraordinary at the time to find a brand-new department established on my own turf without my being consulted. And such a specialized department at that. Mr. Sommers, I understand you have your own way of doing things over there, but here we find it best to take on a new line only after a careful study of the market and consultation with all the parties involved." Meaning him. "I did try to suggest caution at the time."

Yeah, I guess he did at that. "Is it Mrs. Ainsley then? Is she the problem?"

All the way across the Atlantic I could hear Sprogg choosing his words carefully. "Mrs. Ainsley's intentions are above reproach," he finally said. "But sometimes I suspect she overestimates her own knowledge. She loves rare books, there's no doubt of that. Unfortunately, a love of one's specialty doesn't automatically guarantee proficiency. And you did give her virtually autonomous powers, Mr. Sommers. She has been investing heavily in items she's convinced will return a profit. But, ah, she's, how shall I say, misjudged before—"

"You mean she's in over her head."

"I'm afraid so. Frankly, I feel most uneasy, having to rely on her investments to bring our overall profit picture back up to its normal level."

Damn the woman. "Suggestions?"

"Mrs. Ainsley has invested too heavily for us to write the department off as a loss. The only solution I can see is to bring in a bona fide expert and see what he can salvage."

"Have you started looking for one?"

Sprogg admitted that he had. "But rare books experts are almost as rare as the books they handle. The few I found who were even remotely interested said they would come only as department head. They refused absolutely to serve as assistant to someone who doesn't really know the field."

"Then fire her," I said. "Get her out of there."

Sprogg was shocked. "Oh, I couldn't do that. Mrs. Ainsley has been with us for eighteen years. She was a good general agent before, ah, before the rare books. I can't dismiss her out of hand."

"Then ease her out, Sprogg. Get her back to doing her old work and bring in someone who knows what's what. How you handle it is your business—but find a way to handle it. And find it soon."

"I'll do what I can," he said doubtfully.

I hung up, disgusted with this turn of events. The woman had convinced me completely—I'd thought she knew her stuff.

So the man you couldn't fool had been right once again; Amos Speer had said something like this would happen. I should have let it alone.

I'd rented a small furnished apartment instead of relying on motel rooms. She was waiting for me when I got there.

"I was beginning to think you'd changed your mind," she smiled at me.

"Am I late? Sorry. I didn't realize."

"My watch is probably fast," she said accommodatingly.

We were being polite. June looked calm, far calmer than I felt. She wasn't going to lose her poise over something as mundane as taking a midday sex break with her boss.

She'd fixed a shaker of martinis; the perfect secretary. When I'd figured out June must be the one who was helping Wightman, my first impulse had been to fire her. But that wouldn't have been too smart. I had a feeling June could be very useful. Somehow Wightman had won her allegiance; it was up to me to win it back. Since I didn't really know what she wanted, all I could think of was sexual flattery. Besides, I'd always wanted to see what June Murray looked like with her hair mussed up and her make-up smeared and her clothing rumpled.

I tasted the martini: too sweet. "Perfect," I said. "How do you like the apartment?"

"Very attractive. How long have you had it?"

"Three days." Got that, sweetie? The place was rented just for you.

The first time was a bit strained; the second went a little better. June wasn't exactly submissive in bed, but she let me do all the work. Afterwards I forced myself to lie still for the mandatory postcoital chitchat; maybe I could learn something. I led the conversation around to what she really wanted out of life.

"Good work, good health, good friends." It sounded memorized.

"That's all?"

She laughed. "There's something else?"

"Are you happy doing secretarial work?"

But she didn't take the bait. June was too smart to start asking for things after only one session in bed.

We were both playing roles. I was the conventional lecherous employer who took it for granted that secretaries were put on this earth to service their bosses in any way demanded of them. June was the female servant whose only purpose in life was making her master comfortable. And if you think June Murray was type-cast, you believe in Santa Claus.

For several days I'd been noticing a man loitering around the entrance to the gallery. He was there when I arrived in the morning and there when I left at night. Once he was seated in a parked car; the other times he was just standing on the sidewalk. He made no effort to appear like a casual passerby; he was just there, watching. The unsettling part was that he looked vaguely familar.

Then one Friday morning it hit me: he was the voiceless sergeant who'd been with Lieutenant D'Elia during the investigation of Amos Speer's murder. I called police headquarters and asked for D'Elia.

"Are you having me watched?" I demanded when he came on the line.

"Why do you ask that, Mr. Sommers?"

"You know damned well why I ask that. That man of yours, Sergeant whatsisname—he's been out front every day this week."

"Sergeant Pollock. Yes, I posted him there."

"You *posted* him? Why?"

"We still have an unsolved murder on the books, remember," he said unhelpfully.

"So how is watching Speer's front entrance going to solve it?"

"You never know what might turn up. By the way, you might like to hear that your security guards are meticulous about not letting unauthorized visitors into the gallery. Sergeant Pollock was most impressed."

"Meaning he couldn't get in?"

A low chuckle came over the wire. "Now, Mr. Sommers, I think you know we can gain access any time we wish. But we don't want to disturb you any more than we have to."

"Well, you are disturbing me, Lieutenant DEE-lia," I said, deliberately mispronouncing his name. "A cop very obviously watching the entrance all day? You think that's not disturbing?"

"Duh-LEE-uh," he corrected pleasantly. "I'm sorry you're disturbed. I'll tell Pollock to be more discreet."

I slammed the receiver down; I wasn't getting anywhere this way. It seemed incredible to me that the police didn't have anything better to do than stand around all day watching the front entrance of Speer's. What did D'Elia hope to accomplish?

Maybe he'd already accomplished it: he'd rattled me. Maybe D'Elia just wanted to remind me, once again, that he was keeping an eye on me. Still watching. Still not letting me off the hook. Did the Pittsburgh police really have so much manpower they could afford to waste a sergeant on watching a building all day just so he'd be seen twice?

Wait a minute—maybe he didn't watch all day. If the purpose of his being there was to throw a scare into me, then Pollock needed to be visible only when I arrived and when I left. I hurried down to the front entrance and out into the street.

The January wind told me I should have grabbed my coat. I looked both ways down the street; no sign of Pollock. I looked into the parked cars; nobody. I double-checked, then went back inside. Sergeant Pollock was there only at times I could be expected to see him. He'd been sent there to intimidate me.

Lieutenant D'Elia didn't have anything on me. He wouldn't be playing these half-assed games if he did. *In cases where hard evidence is lacking, apply psychological pressure*—did police manuals actually print things like that? He couldn't get me; I was safe. I kept telling myself that. It didn't help much. Just knowing you're suspected by the police is all it takes to throw your digestive processes permanently out of whack. And it was so damned unfair. I didn't kill Amos Speer. Charlie Bates did.

Peg McAllister was waiting in the outer office when I got back. "Got a minute, Earl? A decision needs to be made."

Then make it, I felt like saying. Instead I told her to come on in.

"It's these agreements with Wightman's victims," Peg said. "Going pretty well, on the whole. Most of them are so delighted to be handed extra money that they sign on the spot. But a few are making trouble noises. They don't want to settle for an estimate."

We were up against the problem of figuring out just how much each piece of purloined porcelain was worth. I'd told Peg that Wightman and I had reached an agreement; we would reimburse the people he'd bilked and he would pay us back in installments. I'd said he couldn't help us in determining the value of the porcelain because he'd destroyed all his records to avoid incriminating himself. So Peg and I had hit on the plan of paying off on the basis of what similar pieces of porcelain had sold for recently. And now Peg was saying there were a few soreheads who wanted to know *exactly* what their pieces had gone for.

"So," Peg concluded, "we're going to have to decide whether we want to try to trace their porcelain for them, or continue bargaining in the hope that they'll back down."

I groaned. "Which would cost more?"

"No way of telling. Tracing the porcelain could be an expensive undertaking, or we might get lucky and find what we need straight off. The bargaining might stretch out so long that the final settlements get inflated all out of proportion, or we might reach agreement next week. There's no way to know."

Hell. "What do you suggest?"

"Continue the bargaining. Just to avoid using two different standards for reaching agreement."

I nodded. "Okay, that's what we'll do, then." One decision was as bad as another. "Take care of it, will you?"

When Peg had left, I pulled out the last quarterly reports from the branches and went over them for the hundredth time. I just couldn't find any way of diverting profits from the Rome and Munich branches into what I now thought of as the Wightman Sucker Fund. Not to mention the Sommers Sucker Fund. There were all sorts of ways of juggling books, but I had to make Peg think there was money coming in periodically from Wightman. If I suddenly denied her access to the books, she'd get suspicious.

If worse came to worst, I could always sell my chairs. Holding back the Duprée until last. That would bring in the money, but it would go on the books as profit from normal business deals since the chairs legally belonged to Speer Galleries and not to me personally. Damn it to hell, why should I have to give up my chairs? But with profits down it could easily come to that. But say I did that; say I sold my chairs and made everything right with the people on the sucker lists. Peg would still start wondering when Wightman was going to start paying off. And Peg wasn't a person to leave loose ends lying around.

Peg was the stumbling block. If she'd just keep her nose out of this, I could handle it. I started thinking it was about time for Peg McAllister to retire.

"His name is Arthur Simms," Valentine said. "He's a financial advisor with Keystone Management Consultants. Harvard Business College, positions with various management firms in Oklahoma City, Denver, Chicago, Atlanta. Came to Keystone two years ago. Each move involved a sizable increase in salary. Forty years old, married, two children."

Arthur Simms. Good name for a playmate.

"They meet regularly in an apartment in Shadyside. Mrs. Sommers rented it under an assumed name."

My mouth dropped open. That was the same section of town where I'd rented an apartment to meet June. I asked Valentine for the exact address. He told me; only five or six blocks from my place. Christ.

"How regularly do they meet?" I asked.

"At least twice a week, sometimes three times."

We were sitting in a bar. I didn't want Valentine coming into my office in case Peg should happen to see him and wonder what he was working on now. (Peg again!) The detective droned on, giving me more details about the man Simms. "He's respected in professional circles—his specialty is advising companies that are in financial difficulties. In his personal life his reputation seems to be equally high. So far as I could determine, this is his first extramarital affair. Either that, or he is extraordinarily discreet."

"Pictures," I said. "I want pictures."

Valentine shook his head. "I don't think that will be possible. Mrs. Sommers and Mr. Simms never meet anywhere except at the apartment. They enter and leave separately. I can get pictures of her going into the building, but that's about all. Presumably they did meet publicly early in their relationship, but not now."

"Bug the place. Bust in and catch them in the act."

Valentine smiled politely. "That would cost us our license, Mr. Sommers. And evidence obtained in that manner would not be admissible in court. Certainly not in Pennsylvania. Am I correct in assuming you wish to accumulate evidence for a divorce action?"

"Probably. I haven't decided yet."

"If that's the course you decide upon, your best chance is a mutual consent divorce. What evidence we have is all arguable. Our past experience has been that more concrete evidence than what we have is required to prove adultery. If Mrs. Sommers would agree—"

"Mutual consent—I don't know."

"You can sue for unilateral divorce, of course—one partner seeking release from the marriage contract without the consent of the other. And without having to prove marital misconduct."

"That's the three-year law, isn't it?"

Valentine nodded. "You'll not only have to wait three years after filing your suit before a divorce is granted, you'll also be required to seek marital counseling during that period as well. Three years is a long time to wait—a lot of things can happen. The law is still new enough that all the loopholes haven't been explored yet. Those three years could conceivably drag out much longer. You really should talk to an attorney about this."

"I suppose," I said, discouraged.

Valentine cleared his throat. "Mr. Sommers, may I make a suggestion? The fastest way to get a divorce is still to establish residence in another state. Buy some property in Alabama and find a small-town judge who's not too particular. It's faster and neater than trying to get a divorce in Pennsylvania."

I said I'd consider his suggestion.

"Do you wish me to continue surveillance?" Valentine asked.

I told him yes. He thanked me for his drink and left.

Valentine had pretty much scotched my half-formed notion of getting Speer Galleries away from Nedda through a divorce action. Nedda could move in with her lover for all I cared; in fact, that might even work to my advantage. If she became so besotted with him that she wanted to make him Mr. Nedda number three, then she might be willing to sign over her shares of Speer's just to get me to agree to a divorce. And Arthur Simms's wife would have to be bought off too.

Arthur Simms. My successor? The trouble was I couldn't visualize Nedda getting *besotted* over anybody. But that didn't mean she wouldn't be willing to trade me in on a new model. First Mrs. Speer, then Mrs. Sommers, next Mrs. Simms? Nedda must have had an aversion to changing her monogram.

One thing about Arthur Simms bothered me: his profession. He was a financial advisor, Valentine had said, and a good one. All along I'd been worried that Nedda would get it into her head to run Speer Galleries herself. How better to go about it than to have an expert in advising financially troubled companies at her beck and call? Not that Speer's was in trouble. There were problems, yes, but they could be solved. All I needed was a little time.

Nedda didn't know profits had slipped the last quarter. I hadn't told her and my next annual report to the board wasn't due until the following January. Nor did Nedda know we stood to lose a pile because of Wightman. Peg McAllister knew about Wightman, and I think she suspected about the profits. So somehow I was going to have to make sure Nedda and Peg never sat down for a nice girlish chat. And it wouldn't hurt to keep Nedda and June Murray as far apart as possible, for obvious reasons. Something else—if June was still in cahoots with Wightman, she'd know that story I gave Peg about Wightman's paying us back in installments was a bunch of bull. Which meant that if June and Peg ever got together—my god, they had me coming and going. Maybe I should draw myself a flow chart.

But the main thing was to keep Nedda in ignorance of Speer's temporary financial problems. I'd just about made up my mind to start selling the chairs; I still had to figure out a way to deal with Peg. One thing at a time.

I drove back to the gallery. June wasn't in the outer office; I pushed open my office door and stopped, surprised.

Nedda looked up from the cherrywood table; she held the quarterly reports in her hands. "Not doing so hot, are we?" she said dryly.

11

So I ended up telling Nedda about Wightman after all. I gave her the same version I'd given Peg, that Wightman would repay us in installments. It's better this way, I told her. No publicity.

"Why didn't you tell me about this before?"

"Hey," I laughed, "how about a word of praise or even just a thank you? I uncovered a potentially dangerous situation and I'm dealing with it."

"Why didn't you tell me?" Nedda repeated.

"Because I didn't want you to worry about it. It's ugly."

"That's odd," Nedda said. "You don't usually show me that kind of consideration. And Wightman's chicanery hardly explains this drop in profits the London branch shows. What about that?"

I explained that Deborah Ainsley, the rare books woman, had made some questionable investments and even now was in the process of being replaced.

"Rare books?" Nedda said sharply. "Since when has Speer's been dealing in rare books?"

So my loving wife fancied herself a businesswoman, did she? "An experiment," I said, "which the London branch manager didn't control carefully enough." I talked on, minimizing the whole business. I couldn't tell from her face whether I'd convinced her or not.

"At least the Pittsburgh office seems to be doing all right," she said. "Not exactly setting the world on fire, but all right."

"Of course," I said confidently. "What did you expect?" The reason the Pittsburgh quarterly report was "all right" was that all the chairs in the Fox Chapel house were included as assets. But once I'd sold them and used the money to pay off those good folk on the sucker lists, Pittsburgh's financial picture would change considerably. Next quarter we'd show a loss. But I saw no reason to point that out to Nedda.

The very next day I started making arrangements for selling the chairs. Not all of them at once, and not the Duprée at all, if I could avoid it. I decided which chairs were to be put up for auction, which ones had a chance for a good private sale. I sent a few of the chairs I'd bought in France to the San Francisco branch, including the Egyptian monstrosity. I thought it had a better chance of finding a home out there.

The first returns were a little disappointing. ("You bought too high," Robin Coulter told me bluntly.) Early days yet. But Wightman's sucker list was growing shorter; every one of those creeps was being paid off. Soon I could start on my own list.

One day, as casually as I could, I asked Peg McAllister if she was thinking of retiring soon.

She turned a shocked face toward me. "Why? Why do you ask?"

I tried to speak soothingly. "Speer's has no mandatory retirement age, you know. But Peg, you'll be sixty soon, and that's about the time people start thinking about retirement. I just want to know if you've started thinking about it yet."

Her face took on an expression I can only describe as a declaration of war. "I'm good for another ten years yet! What are you doing, talking to me about retirement?"

I retreated, all the way. "Peg, I just want to make sure I can count on your being here to see me through this Wightman mess. I don't want you to start thinking of rose-covered condominiums when there are still so many loose ends to tie up."

She relaxed. "Is that all? Don't worry. I'll be here 'til the cows come home."

That's what I was afraid of. "Good," I said.

So she wasn't going to allow herself to be eased out. Peg was a shrewd old gal; if she ever became suspicious, I could have trouble on my hands. It wasn't just that I'd lied to her about Wightman, although that was part of it. When she saw the next quarterly report, she was going to start asking questions. And there was always the danger that somehow she might get on to my own list of suckers. (June could tell her, if she ever got mad at me.) Peg had already demonstrated once before that whenever she had to choose between Speer Galleries and Earl Sommers, Earl Sommers could be counted on to come in a very poor second indeed. Peg's all-seeing eye could be a danger; I'd have to watch her.

Unbidden, a memory floated into my mind: Charlie Bates, sitting on a bench by the yak pens, offering to do me a favor. I pushed the memory aside. It wouldn't be necessary.

I hoped.

One morning Nedda casually mentioned that she was meeting a friend named Sharon for lunch. Too casually.

Valentine had said that Nedda and her lover never met in public, but why would she be telling me about a lunch date with a woman friend now? Nedda never bothered keeping me informed of her during-the-day social engagements. So why this time?

"You remember Sharon, don't you?" Nedda asked me. "Tall blonde, bit of a weight problem?"

"Can't say I do. Was she at the wedding?"

Nedda nodded. "She's been in Canada since then. This is the first time I've seen her since she got back."

Fascinating. I really wanted to know about Sharon's sojourn in Canada. I tried to match Nedda's casualness. "Where are you meeting?"

"Murphy's Back Room."

I laughed. "You'll be there all day."

She shrugged. "The food's good. We're in no hurry."

She was making it easy for me. Murphy's Back Room was located in Gateway Towers, a building complex only ten minutes from Speer Galleries. It was as if Nedda were inviting me to check up on her.

I decided to accept the invitation. If Nedda suspected I knew she was having an affair with some pencil-pusher named Arthur Simms, then this was exactly the kind of thing she'd come up with to make me think I was wrong. Arouse my suspicions, let me check up and find her in a totally innocent situation, and then watch me feeling foolish. She and Artie Baby could have a good laugh about it afterward.

But I had some doubt as to how her little scenario was supposed to play. Was I to let her see me at the restaurant? Awkward confrontation, ill-concealed embarrassment, blah blah blah. Or was I supposed to feel so ashamed I'd slink away with my tail tucked between my legs? Improvisation would have to be the order of the day.

So at one o'clock I entered Gateway Towers and glanced into the Back Room and spotted Nedda at a table with a woman I didn't remember ever having seen before. I went into the bar and drank my lunch, keeping an eye on the door all the time. At two-thirty Nedda and her convenient friend left. This, I presumed, was my cue to exit too.

But outside the building the two women said goodbye and went their separate ways. I followed Nedda.

She gave a good imitation of a woman with time on her hands. Nedda wandered in and out of stores, ending up at

Saks. She came out carrying a dress box and glanced around with studied casualness. Her eye slid right over me.

Right here, Nedda, right where you want me to be. Now what?

A drink, that was what. It was late afternoon; I'd lost half a day's work because of this silly stunt. Was all this innocent activity supposed to convince me of something?

I followed Nedda into the bar and slipped into a booth at the rear. Nedda didn't see me, oh my what a surprise. I knew now how the scene was to end. I was supposed to be thinking she was there to meet her lover. I was to sit there and stew in my own juice, watching for the appearance of The Other Man. Nedda would let me wait a little while, and then she'd casually get up and walk out—leaving me with egg on my face. Nedda disappointed me; I was hoping for a more dramatic climax.

"Hey, old buddy! Howya doing?"

Jeeeeeeeeeeeeeeeeesus. His voice was so loud every head in the bar turned in our direction. Including Nedda's. About the last thing in the world I needed was any kind of public association with Charlie Bates. Nedda was smiling in our direction; she picked up her glass and started toward the booth.

"Sit down, Charlie," I said with resignation.

He sat, but popped up again when Nedda reached the booth.

"Why, Earl," she said innocently, "I didn't know you were here."

I made room for her in the booth. "Didn't see you come in. Nedda, this is Charlie."

She slid in beside me. "Does Charlie have a last name?"

"Bates," Charlie said, sitting back down. "Charlie Bates."

"Are you one of Earl's business associates?" she sparkled at him across the table.

Charlie grinned at her, openly appreciating her close-up good looks. "No'm. A friend. Me and Earl go a long ways back."

I could sense Nedda's surprise at his way of expressing himself—but Charlie didn't see a thing, of course. "How far back?" Nedda asked.

"Alla way back to school. Peabody High School, 'smatter of fact. Me and Earl been through a lot together."

Nedda was having trouble suppressing her laughter. "Oh? Like what?"

Charlie gave her what he thought was an enigmatic smile. "Things. Y'know."

"No, I don't."

"Just things."

Nedda smiled winningly. "I'll bet you could tell some wild stories if you wanted to."

Charlie laughed haw-haw-haw. "You better believe it."

"Tell me."

With such an attractive audience, Charlie didn't even try to resist. He launched himself on a nostalgia trip, narrating one boyhood escapade after another in his usual subliterate style. He never caught on that Nedda was laughing at him.

The more ignorant Charlie revealed himself to be, the more vivacious Nedda became. She flirted with him shamelessly. In Charlie she'd found the part of my past I'd managed to keep concealed from her up to now, the gutter beginnings I'd spent my entire adult life trying to get away from. Nedda could listen to Charlie and hear an earlier me. She was absolutely delighted.

I leaned back in my corner of the booth and watched the two of them, Charlie showing off for this sophisticated woman who seemed to find him so interesting and Nedda inwardly exulting over this new needle she'd found to use on me. I wondered how amused she'd be if she knew what Charlie did for a living.

Nedda turned toward me, her eyes gleaming. "Earl, you never told me anything about your boyhood."

I smiled blandly. "Didn't think you'd be interested."

"Oh, I'm interested. In fact, I'm fascinated. And if I hadn't met Charlie, I wouldn't have heard any of this! Charlie, you must come to dinner. I want to hear more. What about Friday?"

Charlie looked crestfallen. "I ain't gonna be here Friday. I gotta job to do in New York. Leaving tomorrow."

Nedda looked almost as disappointed as Charlie. "How long will you be there?"

"Can't tell. One of them jobs that might go fast, might not. Y'know."

Nedda fished in her purse for pencil and paper. "Here's our home phone number. Call me the minute you get back. Promise."

"Sure." Charlie took the number and grinned broadly at me. I stared back coldly; he didn't notice.

When Nedda and I got home, it took me several attempts to convince her; but finally I made her understand that if Charlie Bates ever set foot in that house, I'd burn the place down.

After three weeks of playing at love nest, June Murray finally deigned to tell me what she wanted out of life. Hal Downing's job.

"*Downing's* job?" I said, unbelieving. "Hal was a gofer, a lackey. Amos Speer's personal errand boy. You want a job like that?"

"I want to work as your assistant," June called from the bathroom. "Hal Downing was an errand boy because Mr. Speer made him into one. What the job is depends on the people involved."

I lay on the bed and watched her at the bathroom wash basin, scrubbing at a lipstick smear on the white collar of her dress. I'd been in a bit of a hurry this time. "I didn't know I needed an assistant."

June laughed. "You do, you know. There are a lot of small decisions and detail work I could take off your hands. I'm already doing some of it."

And I hadn't even noticed, shame on me. "And lose the best secretary a man ever had?"

"Anybody can type and take dictation." She came out of the bathroom, looking at the dress collar in a different light. "It's not coming out."

"I'm sorry. Didn't mean to get carried away."

She gave me a small smile. "You're a musser, Earl."

"A what?"

"A musser. You enjoy mussing me up."

I didn't like that. "I don't see how you can say that. It wasn't deliberate."

"Not consciously, perhaps." She went back into the bathroom and resumed scrubbing at the collar.

Don't you just love it when someone drops a line like that on you and than walks away? I resisted as long as I could and then said, "All right, I'll bite. What do you mean, not consciously?"

"I mean you have some subconscious need to see me at a disadvantage."

I lit a cigarette. I didn't understand her strategy. Here she'd just asked me for a promotion and now she was following up by pointing out some serious flaw in my character. "You misjudge me," I said coldly.

I could see her shrug, as if it didn't matter. "You do need an assistant, you know." She slipped the dress over her head and came back into the bedroom. "I can read figures, Earl. I know Speer's isn't doing as well as it should. Part of the trouble is that you've assumed too big a burden. You've never delegated any of your authority. And I'm the logical one to help carry the load."

I lay on my back and blew smoke at the ceiling. She was right, in a way. I could use some help, but help from someone I knew I could rely on. I didn't trust June Murray one inch. On the other hand, June's silent partnership with Leonard Wightman just might be something I could exploit. If June were promoted and made to feel important, she might give me the line I needed to get that bastard. "All right," I said, deciding. "You've got the job."

Whatever her strategy was, it worked.

The Egyptian horror sold in San Francisco for a healthy profit. None of the other chairs did.

We weren't losing money on the chairs; it was just that I'd been counting on a much higher return than we were getting. All of Wightman's victims had been paid off except for two holdouts; Peg assured me they both were just haggling and would come around in time. Selling off the chairs did have one advantageous side effect: things were more pleasant at home. Nedda saw my moving the chairs out of the Fox Chapel house as a concession to her.

Now that Wightman's sucker list was virtually cleared up, I could start thinking about my own. And what I started thinking was that maybe I'd panicked for no reason. It'd been almost three months since Wightman's detective must have completed his investigation of me, but I still hadn't heard from a single one of the people whose ignorance I'd turned into a profit for myself. Not one nasty letter from a lawyer, not even one phone call. Nothing. For a couple of months I'd lived in daily fear that I'd hear from some disgruntled seller who'd say, "Hey, that bowfront chest you told me wasn't a Sheraton—whaja sell it for?" But it didn't happen. And if it hadn't happened by now, it wasn't going to happen. I was safe, I must be. I didn't need to pour a lot of Speer Galleries money into those idiots' bank accounts. All I had to do was keep calm and make rational decisions.

But money was still the problem. We just weren't making enough of it. Even without the payoffs, the picture didn't look good. What I needed was one big sale, one that all by itself would keep us out of the red. It'd have to be a biggie, all right. I'd have to sell something rare and dramatic and highly, highly desirable.

The time had clearly come to auction the Duprée chair. It galled me—god, how it galled me! But I was going to have to do it. I knew I was lucky to have that ace in the hole, but I hated giving the Duprée up so soon. Less than a year I'd had it—not nearly long enough. There's just no way to explain what having a chair like that means.

But once I'd made up my mind to let it go, I kind of looked forward to the excitement. What a fuss the Duprée would cause! I'd checked on the other known Duprée chairs and found there were only eleven of them—all in European museums. For a twelfth to show up on this side of the Atlantic—well, that would set the antiques world on its ear. *The Twelfth Duprée,* that's what our brochure would be titled. Earl Sommers of Speer Galleries is pleased to announce, etc. Every major dealer and museum in Europe and North America would be represented in Pittsburgh. Plus a few egomaniacal billionaire collectors. Yes, the Duprée would get me out of my hole. Selling it was the right thing to do, the right choice to make. That's all I had to do: keep calm, make rational decisions.

So then I made one totally irrational decision, one I'd postponed making because I knew what I ought to do but just couldn't bring myself to do it. I'd lost a lot of sleep because of it. Because of what? Because of an eighteenth-century porcelain figurine standing only seven inches high. The Meissen Leda.

I had in my possession, courtesy of Charlie Bates, a piece of hard evidence linking me directly to the murder of Amos Speer. I couldn't take it home; there was no place there immune to Nedda. I couldn't even bury it in the grounds; one of the gardeners might notice the earth had been disturbed and decide to investigate. I'd been keeping the Leda in the safe in my office—but all Lieutenant D'Elia had to do was get a search warrant and that would be the end of The Story of Earl Sommers, His Rise and Fall. Selling it was out of the question; I couldn't risk its being traced to me. The only sensible thing to do was smash it and scatter the pieces in the Allegheny River.

But I kept putting it off. The figurine was worth four or five thousand dollars, but that wasn't it. The Leda was such a lovely piece—the delicacy of the female figure balanced so exactly by the strength of the swan. A thing of beauty and a joy forever—destroying it would be sacrilege. But that wasn't really it either. The Leda certainly carried a lot of bad associations for me. It was the piece Amos Speer had used in the first step of a squeeze play he'd worked on me. And just as Charlie Bates had said, it was a "souvenir" of a murder. Besides, the word *porcelain* had virtually become synonymous to me with the word *Wightman*, a name guaranteed to bring a vile taste to any moderately sensitive person's mouth. But still I couldn't bring myself to destroy the figurine.

Simply because the Leda and I were both still here. In spite of all the bad associations, in spite of all the things that had gone wrong—the figurine and I had both survived. I was on pretty shaky ground and I could fall any time, but so far I was still on my feet. Speer was dead, Wightman was gone, and Charlie Bates was staying out of my life. I knew I was indulging in symbol-making, but the Meissen Leda had become my trophy of survival. I couldn't destroy that.

There was only one place I could think of where it ought to be safe: the Shadyside apartment I'd rented for meeting June. The place had a brick fireplace in the living room, so one day in late February I got to work. I pried bricks loose until blisters started to form on my hands. The metal box I'd carefully packed the Leda in was small, but it still took a lot of digging and gouging to make a niche large enough. I put in the box and mortared most of the bricks back into place. I cleaned up the mess and got rid of the leftover bricks.

When the mortar had dried, I went back with a shoebox full of dirt I'd burst my blisters digging up from the hard winter ground. I rubbed dirt into the mortar until it took on fairly much the same coloration as the rest of the fireplace wall. If you stood up close and squinted your eyes, you could tell the difference. But from a few feet back, the part I'd patched blended in nicely with the rest of the brickwork. The real test, of course, was June Murray's next visit to the apartment. June's eyes were always working; she didn't miss much. If she couldn't see the difference, then I could feel sure the hiding place was okay.

She didn't notice a thing. Or else she noticed it and didn't think it worth mentioning. After all, what was one more patch in a brick wall? One thing I did *not* have to worry about was her digging out the bricks herself to see if something valuable was concealed behind them. June didn't like getting her hands dirty.

In March I made a mistake. I sent Robin Coulter to another Mercer auction in New York.

This was the fourth she'd attended. By then the Mercer people had gotten to know her and they liked her style. They offered her a position, she accepted, and that was that.

"Don't I even get a chance to match their offer?" I said when she told me.

"No point, Earl. My husband and I have been thinking about pulling up stakes for some time now. The Mercer offer just made it easy."

"Are you that eager to get away from Pittsburgh?"

"Well, yes," Robin laughed. "As a matter of fact, we are. Jim's caught in a dead-end job and I, well, I'm ready to move on, let's say."

"Oh, let's do say that," I answered sarcastically. "Speer's is honored to have been used as a rest stop."

"If it's a rest stop, you've made it one," she shot back. Now that she was no longer working for me Robin saw no need to keep up the pretense of friendliness.

"Speer's is ten times the size of Mercer's," I said. "You've demoted yourself."

"I don't think so. Earl, it's just not the same here since Mr. Speer died. You've changed the whole nature of the business—and not for the better. I'm telling you this for your own good."

"Of course," I murmured. "Why else?"

"We can't go out and deal the way we used to. Now we always have to keep in mind what *you* might like. I know of at least six good buys you turned down just because you didn't like those particular styles. Earl, that's no way to run a business!"

"How old are you, Robin? Twenty-seven, twenty-eight?"

"I'm thirty, but you don't have to be old and gray to know you can't run an antiques business as if it were a personal hobby. One reason I've leaving is that I no longer believe Speer's is going to go on forever."

"Why didn't you tell me all this sooner?" I said. "Surely you knew I'd have been delighted to let you tell me how to run the business."

"And that's the other reason I'm leaving," she blazed. "I'm sick and tired of trying to be nice to you. Earl, you're the hardest person to be nice to I know! You with your conceit and your roving hands and your self-indulgence—ah, what's the use." She threw up her hands in surrender. "You hear what you want to hear, you see what you want to see. There's no talking to you." Then Robin Coulter turned her back on me and walked away.

So goodbye, Bedroom Eyes. And to hell with you, you frigid little bitch.

12

My announcement that a hitherto undiscovered Duprée chair would be offered in open auction on May first created a most gratifying furor. Requests for *The Twelfth Duprée* (our brochure) came pouring in, many of them from dealers and small museums that could never afford to be in on the bidding. They just wanted to know about the chair. The Duprée would be on display the entire month of April; the Metropolitan Museum of New York and the Louvre had been among the first to make appointments to examine it.

All this to-do meant extra security, extra insurance. The insurance man turned dead white when he learned I'd been keeping the chair in the Fox Chapel house for nearly a year. When I told him I'd put on an extra security guard, he just shook his head at me in disbelief. Oh well, the chair hadn't been stolen and it certainly was well protected now. Security guards stood twenty-four-hour watch in the showroom.

Even Nedda got caught up in the excitement. Since the beginning of the year she'd been taking little two- or three-day trips ("Just to get out of Pittsburgh for a while"). I wondered what Arthur Simms had been telling his wife to explain his frequent overnight absences. When Valentine came up with evidence that Nedda and her lover had registered as man and wife in a New York hotel, I told him to discontinue the surveillance. I had all I needed.

But with all the attention being paid to Speer Galleries because of the Duprée, Nedda started staying home more. She found success attractive, and I was beginning to look like a winner again. Nedda was one of those people who give you their wholehearted support every time you no longer need it.

"Who do you think will get it?" Nedda asked me one day in the showroom.

"Either the Louvre or the Metropolitan," I said. "My money's on the Met."

"Why?"

"Because the Louvre already has two Duprées and the Metropolitan doesn't have any. It's a matter of national pride, as well as a question of having the funds to stay in the bidding. The French will think they have a moral right to the chair because it's part of their artistic heritage. But the Met wants to be the only museum in this country with an authentic Duprée on display—and that's a powerful incentive. Besides, for sheer orneriness in expanding its acquisitions, nobody can beat the Met."

The chair had occupied the place of honor in the Fox Chapel house for almost a year, but Nedda was looking at it as if she'd never seen it before. "How much will it bring?"

"Hard to say. But I wouldn't be surprised if it set a record for the highest amount ever paid for a single chair. Interest has been even greater than I thought it'd be. Middle six figures, I'd guess."

Nedda laughed softly and shook her head. "All that money. For a chair. A place to rest your butt." The security guard stationed by the Duprée shot her a startled look and then looked away quickly.

I was equally startled. "You can't be serious. You don't really think the Duprée's just something to sit on, do you?"

She grimaced. "Please, no little lectures about artistic values. It's a lovely chair, of course. But can you look me in the eye and claim the *art* in that chair is worth hundreds of thousands of dollars?"

Her obtuseness so stunned me I could only come back with a cliché. "You can't put a monetary value on art."

She laughed in delight. "Why, Earl, you do it every day of your life! And you do it by muddying the line between art and rarity. That's where the money is—in rarity. If only one urinal were left in the world it would be universally acclaimed as the most exquisite work of art known to western civilization."

I was the one who'd come out of the slums but my well-bred wife could be as crude as they make them. "Don't knock it, kiddo," I said. "It's what pays your bills."

"You think I don't know that?" she grinned. "Earl, I don't think you're being very realistic. All I'm saying is the primary reason the Met wants that chair is to lord it over other American museums. The art is secondary."

"You don't know what you're talking about," I told her bluntly. "You have no understanding of this business and you shouldn't be so quick to pass judgment. Better leave business matters to me."

The laugh disappeared from her face and her voice. "I know more about what goes on here than you think I do. And don't tell me to mind my own business. This *is* my business, remember?"

Pennsylvania crude. "I have work to do," I said and left her standing there. It was a retreat, but the security guard was finding it harder and harder to pretend he wasn't listening.

My new secretary looked up as I went charging through the outer office. "Mrs. McAllister just called. She—"

"Get her back, will you?"

My new secretary was male. Quiet, deferential, efficient. A pleasant young man—June Murray had selected him. June herself had wrinkled her nose in distaste at the windowless cubicle that had been Hal Downing's office. She'd done some reassigning of space and ended up in a corner rm w rv vw.

Buzz, buzz. "Mrs. McAllister."

"Peg?"

"Good news, Earl. The last two holdouts have settled. Now every one of those people Wightman bilked has been taken care of."

So at last it was finished. That was one nightmare I could stop wrestling with. Then Peg gave me the bad news: the final tab came to four hundred ten thousand dollars. It could have been worse, I guess. But not much. Pins under his fingernails. Boiling oil.

"By the way," Peg was saying, "isn't it about time for that crook to start paying you back? Have you gotten any money out of him yet?"

"Not until July," I said hastily. "That was the agreement."

"You should have gotten it in writing," she grumbled and hung up.

Peg and I had almost come to blows when she learned I had no signed agreement with Wightman. I'd told her he'd refused outright to sign anything, that he was willing to go along with the repayment scheme only if I could guarantee we'd keep his name clean. We'd told his victims there'd been a "mistake" in the original evaluations. Lie upon lie upon lie. It had been all I could do to keep Peg from charging out to San Francisco herself to get the agreement down in black and white, all legal and proper. Things had been a bit cool between us for a few days after that. Peg was definitely becoming a nuisance.

But I'd just given myself another couple or months. I'd think of something by then.

I'd barely had a moment to revel in the good feeling of being free of Wightman's sucker list when June Murray came in with a scheme. She wanted me to let her set up a new department—to handle memorabilia.

"Shirley Temple drinking mugs at twenty-five dollars each?" I scoffed. "You're joking. Penny-ante stuff."

"Not if it's handled in volume. Switching to volume dealing would take some reorganizing, but we could manage it without too much expense."

"Oh June, no."

"Wait—hear me out. Two years ago everyone was saying the memorabilia craze had already peaked, but it just wasn't true—it's stronger today than ever. Earl, it's not only the rich who have the urge to collect. There are a lot of people out there who can't afford to invest heavily in antiques but who are quite willing to plunk down a few dollars for an old country store sign or a Mickey Mouse pull toy. It's a good source of income, and we're not taking advantage of it."

"Out of the question," I said shortly. "Speer's doesn't deal in schlock. I'm surprised at you, June. We don't even handle art nouveau anymore."

And that's another mistake, her expression said. "At least promise me you'll think about it."

"No," I said, "I won't promise you I'll think about it. It's *junk*, June!"

"Of course it's junk. It's also money."

"No. Absolutely not. Never."

"Well, that sounds definite," she said dryly.

"As definite as I can make it. No memorabilia."

"You're a snob, Earl," she said, but she smiled when she said it. "All right, if you've made up your mind. But do you really think it's wise to handle only those pieces that measure up to your personal standards of quality?"

"A Mickey Mouse pull toy is a better standard?"

"I didn't make myself clear. We can't deal only in items you like personally. That would be nice, but it's not very sound business. Earl, you need another source of income. If you're so dead set against memorabilia, then let's find something else. At least think about *that*."

"Three weeks my new assistant has been on the job," I told the ceiling. "And already she's telling me how to run the business."

June didn't say anything for a moment. Then: "Well, I can't make you listen. All I can do is point to the figures. The Duprée chair is bailing you out this time, but then what?"

"Look, June, you don't understand. I've had unusual expenses—"

"You mean the four hundred thousand you had to pay out to those people Mr. Wightman cheated. Peg calls them 'the greedy children.' I think it was magnanimous of you, Earl—not exposing Mr. Wightman, I mean. Exposure would ruin a man in our business. Any man. Even you."

And that was June Murray's clever little way of letting me know she knew *why* I hadn't exposed Wightman. Subtle, huh? Her expression gave nothing away, but she'd made her point: the squeeze starts here. One damn thing finishes and another begins.

"All right, June," I sighed. "Start looking for a new line we can carry. But not memorabilia, please."

Her victory smile was dazzling. "I'll get on it right away. It's the right step to take, Earl. You'll see."

"Sure."

"And don't worry about it. I'll take care of everything."

I'll bet you will. "Good girl, June."

She threw me an odd look and left.

First Peg pressuring me about Wightman, now June using her knowledge of my double-dealing to blackmail me into letting her encroach upon my authority. And another one at home giving me a hard time every time I turned around. I was beginning to wish Charlie Bates would come in and free me of all my women.

Wightman I wanted to save for myself.

My new secretary looked up from the phone. "It's the guard at the front entrance. He says a Lieutenant D'Elia wants to come in."

I groaned to myself. "Tell him okay." I couldn't very well refuse his admittance. "I'll be in the showroom." Maybe I could avoid him that way.

Duprée Day was fast approaching. The security guards had been provided with the names of the dealers and museum representatives who were authorized to examine the chair. We were auctioning some other good pieces on the same day to take advantage of the enthusiasm generated by the Duprée.

When I got to the showroom I groaned again. There was Lieutenant D'Elia, scrutinizing the object of everybody's concern. Speer's had gotten a lot of good publicity because of that chair. (Even the morning paper had realized something unusual was going on; they'd printed a picture of the chair on the front page, bumping the usual photos of cute kids and puppies.) But I could have done without D'Elia's attention.

"Hello, Lieutenant. What do you think of it?" The friendly approach.

D'Elia dragged his eyes away from the chair. "Frankly, I don't know what to think of it. It's a pretty chair. The paper said the bidding would start at three hundred fifty thousand dollars. Is that right?"

"That's right," I smiled. "That's only the starting point, of course. The very least I expect is five hundred thousand."

He turned his gaze back to the Duprée. "Half a million dollars." He thought about that a minute and then abruptly turned his back on the chair. "Why, Sommers? Why is one chair worth half a million dollars?"

"Because it's a rare work of art," I said simply. "Art isn't confined to easel paintings, Lieutenant." I picked up one of our brochures from a table. "Here, this will tell you something about Duprée. Unfortunately there isn't much of his work around. That's one reason this piece will go so high."

"Half a million," D'Elia muttered as he took the brochure. I didn't tell him I thought the final figure would probably be between six and seven hundred thousand. It might even reach eight. *Too high*, I told myself sharply. Mustn't indulge in wishful thinking.

"Will the chair end up in a museum?" D'Elia wanted to know.

"Almost certainly. Both the Metropolitan and the Louvre are determined to get it. But there might be a dark horse bidder."

"Meaning?"

"I mean an agent in the employ of some eccentric individual collector whose greatest pleasure in life is outbidding museums." I shuddered. "The Duprée could end up in a vault in Saudi Arabia."

D'Elia looked as if he thought that might be a good place for it. "I wanted to ask you, Sommers. Have you heard from Wightman lately?"

I started to say no when the import of what he was asking hit me. "Why, Lieutenant! You mean you don't know everything that's going on here? What happened to your sources of information?"

He shrugged. "We know you went out to San Francisco in January. We know you talked to Wightman."

"But you don't know why, or whether we've talked since." *And it's bugging you.* "No, I haven't heard from him. I went out to suggest a business deal but we couldn't agree on terms. I've had no reason to talk to him since then. Why do you want to know?"

"Let's go to your office."

I led the way. Inwardly I was exulting; promoting June had been the right move. Now that she had a vested interest in Speer's, she wasn't going to blab to the police or anybody else about everything that happened here.

When we were in my office D'Elia said, "All right, I'll tell you. It was Wightman who was my ear inside this place. He contacted me right after Amos Speer's murder. He was convinced you were responsible."

It was *Wightman?* It wasn't June?

Double blow: "He thought *I* killed Speer?"

"He thought you engineered it. Hired someone to do it. Wightman had no evidence, of course. But somehow he'd found out about your, er, friendship with Mrs. Speer and anticipated your taking over the directorship of the business. That gave you a strong motive, of course."

I was so stunned I couldn't think of a thing to say.

"You and Wightman never got along, did you?" D'Elia asked rhetorically. "It seemed clear to me that Wightman's accusation was motivated by spite. Rather waspish man, isn't he? But when everything he predicted would happen *did* happen—your marriage to Mrs. Speer, your taking over the business—well, then I began to take him more seriously."

"You mean now you think I did hire someone to kill Speer?"

"I mean it's a possibility we have to consider."

"Double talk. Lieutenant, I don't even know how to go about hiring a killer. What do you do, advertise for one? You're wrong, you're dead wrong. Why are you telling me about this now? Speer's been dead for over a year."

"The Duprée chair. The last day Amos Speer ever spent in this gallery, he told his secretary he'd just found a genuine Duprée and then he said something rather strange. He said, 'I've got Sommers now.' His secretary mentioned this odd association of 'Duprée' and 'Sommers' to Wightman. Wightman interpreted it to mean there was something fishy going on in connection with the chair, and somehow you were connected with it."

"He would. That's Wightman to a T—always looking for dirt." So June and Wightman were in cahoots even that far back. She hadn't gossiped to the police the way I'd thought, but she was still in that bastard Englishman's camp.

D'Elia said, "What did Speer mean, 'I've got Sommers now'?"

"I have no idea. I don't even know he did say that. You got it third hand, remember. Lieutenant, you've got to understand about Wightman. He likes to make trouble. The man is just plain bad news."

D'Elia was nodding his head. "That was the impression I got. Especially when no Duprée chair was offered for auction. Speer's secretary very conveniently didn't remember the conversation, so I more or less decided Wightman had made the whole story up. Then one morning a year later I open the newspaper and there's a picture of a Duprée chair on the front page. And the story says it's being offered for auction by none other than Speer Galleries. Why so long? Why did you wait a year before auctioning the chair?"

I sighed, knowing this part of it was hopeless. "If you were a lover of antique furniture, Lieutenant, maybe I could make you understand. I just couldn't bring myself to let it go. You have something as special as that Duprée, you don't give it up in a hurry. Oh, I knew I'd have to sell it eventually—it belongs to the gallery, not to me. But I kept putting it off. I hate to see it go now. I'd buy it for myself if I could."

I couldn't tell whether he believed me or not, and that was ironic: it was the only thing I'd told him that was true. "Where did the chair come from?" D'Elia wanted to know. "Another dealer?"

"No, it belonged to a housewife in Beaver Falls. A Mrs. Percy. She didn't even know the chair was valuable."

"So Speer was able to get it cheap?"

"Hardly," I said dryly. "He paid her three hundred thousand for it."

"So where do you come into the story?"

"I made the find. I went to Mrs. Percy's house to look at a table she wanted to sell and just happened to spot the Duprée in another room. I gave her a small deposit to hold the chair until Speer could get out there and take a look himself. The rest is history, as they say. So I really don't know why Speer would have said he'd 'got' me—he was quite pleased about the find. In fact, he'd promised me a bonus. I don't think you appreciate how rare a find it was."

"You can prove legal ownership of the chair, I presume."

"Of course. We don't keep valuable papers in the files—they're all in the bank. You'll need Peg McAllister's signature to see them. I'll have my secretary show you to her office."

For reasons of his own D'Elia accepted his cue. "Well, good luck on the auction. When is it?"

"In four days." I opened the door for him and told my secretary to take him to Peg's office. Then I went back into my own office and quietly collapsed.

I thought I'd handled it all right; D'Elia seemed satisfied. It was a good thing policemen weren't as objective as they were supposed to be. D'Elia hadn't liked Wightman, and that had worked to my advantage. That sonofabitch was behind all my troubles—he'd known about Nedda and me, he'd gone to the police and accused me of murder, he'd blackmailed me into making good on his lousy deals—I was so angry I was shaking. I'd have to stop thinking about Wightman, just put him out of my mind until after the auction. Then I'd give my whole attention to finding a way to *make him pay.* And pay. And pay some more.

It took me nearly an hour to calm down to the point I could concentrate on work again. I was just about ready to call it a day when the phone buzzed.

"M. Guicharnaud to see you."

René Guicharnaud was the representative the Louvre had sent to bid on the Duprée. "Ask him to come in, please." Our code phrase for "Open the door for him and be extra polite."

M. Guicharnaud waited until the secretary had withdrawn and then came straight to the point. In careful and reluctant English, he told me my Duprée chair was a fake.

13

It was the corner blocks that had first tipped M. Guicharnaud off, those wooden wedges inserted into the corners of the chair seat to strengthen the frame. They were too large. I'd known Duprée had used small corner blocks, and the blocks in my chair looked small enough to me. But then I hadn't had two authentic Duprée chairs on hand to establish a basis for comparison. Guicharnaud did. He went on to find a few other questionable things—traces of a glue that may or may not have been contemporary, a suspiciously small amout of wood shrinkage for the supposed age of the chair, etc. One such matter might be dismissed as an individual aberration from what could be expected; but put them all together, they spell fake.

Who had built the fake Duprée? And what had gone so wrong that the imitation ended up languishing in the back bedroom of a tract house in Beaver Falls? We'd probably never know. The chair wasn't totally worthless, but we'd recover only a fraction of the three hundred thousand it had cost. Famous fakes always had a certain curiosity value, and this fake had already earned its place in history as the chair that made a fool out of Speer's. This one was going to be hard to live down.

Nedda responded in her usual sensitive way. "How could you be so stupid?" she asked wonderingly. "Earl, how could you be so *stupid?*"

"Don't blame this one on me," I growled. "It was your dear late husband who shelled out three hundred thousand bucks for an imitation, not me."

"Only because you didn't have three hundred thousand." She went out of the bedroom and came back immediately with a check in her hands. "I found this among Amos's papers. It's a check for five hundred dollars made out to Eleanor Percy—that's the woman in Beaver Falls Amos bought the chair from. Earl, you tried to get the Duprée for yourself."

I put on an express of indignant anger. "That check wasn't even cashed—it was a deposit. To hold the chair until dear Amos could decide what he wanted to do."

"Bullshit," she said bluntly. "You must think I'm a fool—agents don't make deposits for the galleries out of their personal accounts. You tried to cheat us out of what you thought was a lot of money."

That regrouping of forces rocked me more than her accusation. *You*—Earl Sommers. *Us*—Nedda Speer, Amos Speer, Speer Galleries. "If that's what you think," I said carefully, "why did you wait until now to spring it on me?"

"Because everybody steals. I thought if you were in charge, you wouldn't need to anymore. But this fake Duprée changes things. I've suspected for some time I made a mistake—Earl, you're not right for the job."

"Which job?" I asked. "Director of the galleries or Mr. Nedda?"

"No one held a gun to your head," she said evenly. "You made your choices too. But you not only fooled me, you fooled yourself as well. Earl, you're always telling me I don't really *see* these marvelous chairs that set you all atwitter. But you looked at that phony Duprée every day for nearly a year and didn't see a single thing to make you suspicious. You're supposed to be an *expert*, Earl."

"Amos Speer thought it was genuine," I said defensively.

"Yes," she answered softly, "and that made all the difference, didn't it? Amos had a reputation as a man you couldn't fool—and when he agreed the chair was a Duprée, it didn't even occur to you to question his judgment. Even though you already had evidence he *could* be fooled. He never found out Wightman was stealing from him. And he never knew about us."

"You're sure about that, are you?" I said sardonically. "Wightman knew."

That stopped her. "*Wightman* knew?"

"He not only knew, he told Lieutenant D'Elia." I let myself enjoy the moment of discomfort that little revelation caused her.

But she shook it off. "So they knew, so what. The point is, the galleries aren't doing well enough to absorb a three-hundred-thousand-dollar loss right now. Something has to be done."

A seven-hundred-thousand-dollar loss, I silently corrected her. Three for the chair, four for Wightman's victims. "You're about to bust out with a suggestion, I can tell."

"Damned right I am. You need a financial advisor, Earl. Someone versed in the economic realities of profit and loss."

So here it was. "Someone like Arthur Simms?"

She didn't bat an eye. "Arthur can help us. He can find ways to get the galleries back on the right track again."

Greedy Nedda, wanting everything, wanting it all her own way. "Tell the truth, Nedda. You want to run the galleries yourself."

She looked as if she didn't believe her ears. "What did you say?"

"It's what you've always wanted, isn't it? To run the whole show yourself Playing queen over an antiques empire. But it's not play, Nedda—you don't even begin to understand what's involved. You could no more run Speer's than you could swim the English Channel underwater."

She stared at me incredulously for a long time, then barked a short laugh and became suddenly furious. "Earl, you fool—why do you think I married you? I married you so I wouldn't *have* to run the galleries!"

Now I was the one having trouble believing what I was hearing. "You married me—"

"To get a director for Speer's. Amos was getting old and I wanted to have someone ready to take over. Better than putting in a stranger I couldn't control."

"And me you can control. I see."

"I'm not sure you do, but it doesn't matter now. Now all I want is for you to let Arthur Simms come in and find out what's going wrong. A simple, straightforward business procedure. When you're in trouble, you call in an expert. Earl, you need an expert."

I'd been sitting on the side of the bed; now I stretched out on my back and stared at the ceiling. "You're right, Nedda. That's exactly what I need. My wife's lover watching every move I make."

Nedda laughed, a harsh sound. "Don't take that superior line with me. A man who's having an affair with his secretary? Honestly, Earl, how middle-class can you get?"

I was sitting up again, staring at her in astonishment.

"Of course I know about it," she snapped. "I keep telling you I'm not a fool. I know about it and I'd laugh if I weren't so disgusted. Your secretary! Who ends up getting a promotion out of it. You can watch that story on any soap opera. Earl, I didn't shame you by carrying on with, with a tennis pro. But you have no more style than to get involved with your *secretary*. You embarrass me."

This was unreal. In spite of myself I started to laugh. "Let me make sure I've got this straight. You don't object to my having an affair so long as the woman involved meets with your approval? Is that it?"

"It's so trite," she objected. "The whole damned affair is a cliché. *June Murray* is a cliché. Look at her—the perfect secretary, the office wife, the provider of all comforts. I'm surprised other secretaries haven't drummed her out of the corps. And you played along with it—why? Did it make you feel important? Command and it shall be given?"

"Nedda," I said abruptly, "do you want a divorce?"

She took her time answering. "I've been thinking that might not be a bad idea," she said slowly.

"Fine," I said, stretching back out on the bed. "The price is Speer Galleries."

Shocked, she came over to the side of the bed. "Are you *insane?*"

"Never saner. You want out of the marriage? That's what it's going to cost you. We'll make some sort of arrangement so you and the new boy won't go hungry. But the galleries are mine."

"The galleries will *never* be yours," she hissed.

"Then resign yourself to the status quo."

The look on her face made me feel better than I'd felt for months. But she rallied and tried again. "Earl, I will not be blackmailed. I simply won't let it happen. I've already consulted a lawyer and he—"

"Has undoubtedly explained to you all about the three-year wait in a unilateral suit. Did he also tell you it might take even longer? Oh, you can fly down to Haiti or the Dominican Republic and get a quickie. But you know damned well it won't be recognized in Pennsylvania. So face it, you whore, you're stuck."

"*I'm* not the one who sold myself," she said heatedly. "I bought *you*. And a bad bargain it was."

I laughed in her face. "*Caveat emptor.*"

She slammed out of the room. I think I can say I won that one.

I dropped into June Murray's new office. "Any ideas for a new line yet? After this Duprée fiasco we're going to have to find something fast. I may end up agreeing to memorabilia after all."

Instead of answering, June handed me an envelope.

"What's this?"

"My resignation."

Take that! Just when I'd started depending on her . . . "Why, June? I gave you what you wanted."

She gave me her mouth-only smile. "It's a matter of financial security, Earl. I don't see much future for myself here."

"Assistant to the Director isn't good enough?"

She shook her head. "You don't understand. I don't see much future for anybody at Speer's."

Why, the arrogant little . . . "I think you'd better explain that."

"Oh, it's not really necessary, is it? We both know what's happening here. To put it frankly, I want to get out while the getting's good."

"That's just wonderful, June. I always knew I could count on you." I glared at her but she didn't answer. Part of me was relieved at being rid of her, but I wasn't too happy at the thought of June Murray wandering around loose knowing the things she knew. "If it's more money you want—"

"Earl, you can't afford to pay me more money. You can't afford what you're paying me now. I once thought we could build Speer's up together." (Translation: she'd thought *she* could build it up.) "But now I see I was wrong. The mistake about the Duprée is symptomatic of all the things that are wrong here. You're just not Amos Speer, Earl. I'm sorry it worked out this way, but I have to think of my future."

I wondered if she ever thought of anything else. June was a careful woman; she wouldn't be making this move unless she'd already found a new warm place for herself. "Where are you going, June? What are you going to do?"

"I'm going to San Francisco," she said. "Leonard Wightman has offered me a partnership."

A partnership! I'd never thought of that. Not that I ever would have offered one to the two-faced bitch, but Wightman had one-upped me. "Payment for past services?" I snapped. "Or do you have something new to sell?" She just looked at me, saying nothing. I could think of only one more thing to try; I went over and put my arms around her. "Don't do it, June. I want you to stay."

She pushed me away. "Don't be insulting, Earl."

"Insulting? I tell you I want you to stay and that's insulting?"

"You think I'm so weak-headed I'd give up a partnership for the pleasures of going to bed with you? I think that's insulting."

Seemed to me she wasn't the only one being insulted. "All right, June. If you're determined to go, I can't stop you. But we've been close—you just can't pretend that's never happened. So on the basis of that I'm going to ask you to do something for me. Before you go, tell me how I can get Wightman. You've helped him—now help me."

Her face was a study in innocence. "I don't know what you're talking about."

"Think a moment before you say no. If I can discredit Wightman, that would leave you in control of his gallery. You'd like that, wouldn't you? I can help you. Just give me a line on how I can get to him."

She looked at me in frank amazement. "You can't hurt my partner without hurting me too. And Earl, I'm not going to cooperate in my own destruction. I've got a good opportunity and I'm going to take it. There's no way you can talk me out of it."

The bitch. "You overestimate your own value, June," I said coldly. "Your ambition exceeds your capabilities. You must have something on Wightman yourself. It's blackmail, isn't it? That's the only way Wightman would give *you* a partnership."

"Why don't you leave, Earl? This isn't getting us anywhere."

"You're the one who's leaving. Now. This minute. Get your things, June. I'm going to escort you out myself."

That got to her, but she couldn't do anything about it. She'd already made a start at cleaning out her desk, so it didn't take long to gather up her personal belongings. I didn't help her carry them. I took her down to the front entrance and made sure she heard me instruct the security guard that one June Murray was to be denied entrance to Speer's hereafter.

"Good boy, Earl," she said dryly, and left.

Granted, it was an act of petty spite, but it made me feel a lot better. I stood behind the glass doors and watched her make her way down the street. A man spoke to her, but she hurried by without answering. The man was Lieutenant D'Elia, and he had four other men with him. One of them was Sergeant Pollock. Now what.

"A search warrant," D'Elia said, holding up a legal-looking paper. "And I have another for your home."

"What the hell for?" I exploded. "What do you expect to find?"

"The genuine Duprée," he said, and gestured to his men to get started.

I put one hand against the wall to support myself. I didn't know whether to laugh or cry. "Search and be damned," I said weakly.

"Could we go to your office?"

"Can I stop you?" We went to my office.

"I've been doing some reading about antique furniture," D'Elia said when he'd settled himself. "Especially about how to spot fakes. Quite ingenious—the faking, I mean. Like the books say always test the screws. If they loosen easily, then they're not very old. But there's a way around that. All you have to do is put a little water in the screw hole first, and the screw just rusts into place. Won't budge—and it makes the chair appear older than it is. Is that what happened with the Duprée?"

"There are no screws in a Duprée chair."

He looked disappointed. "Well, whatever was done was good enough to fool Amos Speer. And from what I hear he didn't fool easy. Or maybe the chair he bought wasn't a fake. Maybe the fake was put together later. Like during the year between Speer's death and the time you announced the auction."

I just stared at him, so disgusted I could hardly speak. "You think I substituted a fake Duprée for a genuine one."

"That's what I think."

"And then what? Put an ad in the paper—stolen Duprée for sale?"

"There are always buyers for stolen works of art if you know how to find them. And you're in a position to know. Maybe one of those rich eccentrics who hide their treasures in underground vaults."

"If you'd just stop to think, Lieutenant, you'd see how absurd that is. Why would I risk exposing myself and the galleries to ridicule by offering a chair for auction I knew was a fake? Do you have any idea what a setback this is for us?"

"Maybe you don't care about the galleries as much as you claim you do. A private deal on the side would put a lot of change in your pocket. I talked to the Frenchman, ah . . ."

"Guicharnaud."

"Yeah. He said he was authorized to go as high as six hundred thousand. The man from the Metropolitan wouldn't tell me what he was going to bid. But six hundred thousand—that's enough to tempt anybody."

"And you're seriously suggesting I would risk ruining Speer's for six hundred thousand dollars?"

"That's what I'm saying."

"Listen, you dumb cop, you've got it exactly backwards. I would risk six hundred thousand dollars to help Speer's any day of the week, but never the other way around. Never."

"That sounds very noble," D'Elia said sarcastically. "Too bad I don't believe a word of it. Ever since this thing started a year ago, *you've* always been the one to cash in. Nobody else profited, nobody else had anything to gain. Just you. I think you had Speer killed, Sommers. You hired somebody to do it while you were in your office establishing an alibi for yourself. I don't know whether your wife knew about it or not, and I don't much care. *You* were behind it, and I'm going to nail you for it."

"Threats? Intimidation? Does your search warrant grant you Gestapo powers?"

"It was the Duprée chair that had me stumped," he plodded on, unhearing. "All I had to go on was Wightman's suspicions, and he's such a vindictive man I couldn't really trust his opinion. But then you put the chair up for auction and it turns out to be a fake. Then it all started to make sense. Were you hoping it was good enough to fool the experts? Either way, you still stood to make a bundle. Sommers, you're a murderer and a thief, and somewhere there's evidence to prove it. All I have to do is find it. And you can be damned sure I will."

I started to reach for the phone to call Peg McAllister; this mule-headed policeman scared me and I wanted my lawyer with me. But then I changed my mind. D'Elia's men weren't going to find a genuine Duprée because there wasn't any to be found. D'Elia couldn't charge me without evidence. What he thought and what he'd said didn't have to go beyond this room. The less Peg knew about my troubles the better.

The police were still hard at it when I left for the day. I got home to find Nedda virtually shaking with outrage.

"Police," she said in a voice people usually use when talking about cockroaches. "Police crawling all over my home, prying into everything. They even sounded the walls, looking for concealed rooms."

It wasn't exactly welcome-home-darling-how-was-your-day, but it was the first time Nedda had spoken to me since our showdown about the divorce. "I know. It was that way at the gallery too."

"*Police* searching my home! Everything's disintegrating—and now my privacy is violated. Earl, you're the biggest mistake I've ever made in my life. You damage everything you touch."

"Oh, it's *my* fault those idiot police are looking for a chair that doesn't exist? That's my fault?"

"Who else's? They suspect you of something, Earl. There's got to be some reason a squad car full of men waving search warrants roars up to my front door. If they suspect you, they're probably wondering about me. How dare you bring this on me? How dare you?"

So Queen Nedda's dignity was offended; tough. "You really have a lot of sterling qualities, Nedda. Courage, loyalty, grace under pressure—"

"Don't be sarcastic with me," she snarled. "We're both past that now. Look, I can't hang around here and watch this happening. I've got to get out of here for a while. I'm going to New York for a week or two."

"A week or two?" I raised an eyebrow at her. "Will his wife let him out for that long? Well, have fun with your screwing and scheming. It won't do you any good, you know. The price is still Speer Galleries."

She looked at me with something like regret. "You really are hopeless, aren't you?" she said softly.

I didn't answer her. She didn't deserve an answer.

14

The security guard's records showed the police hadn't left until 4 A.M. I hoped they all had trouble staying awake during the day.

Peg McAllister was waiting in my office for me. She looked miserable.

"Sit down, Peg. Why the long face?"

She sat on the edge of a chair, looking depressed as hell. "Earl, this is difficult for me. I have something to tell you."

"Then tell me."

"It's not easy."

"Say it, Peg."

"I've decided to retire."

So. Another one walking out on me. Well, I'd wanted Peg to retire. So why did I feel betrayed? "I see. Too much heat in the kitchen?"

Her face was pinched and drawn. "Try to understand, Earl. Speer Galleries has been my life. I always knew leaving would be agony. But the time has come. And I did stay until the Wightman mess was cleaned up, just as I said I would."

"You also said you'd be here until the cows come home, if I remember right."

"You remember right." She shook her head. "I'm sorry, Earl. I know how this must look. Like desertion under fire. Especially after the disappointment of the Duprée chair. But when that policeman came into my office yesterday with a search warrant, I had to face up to the fact that things were getting worse every day. We're losing money, the phony Duprée made us a laughingstock. And now the police think Speer's knowingly participated in an attempt to defraud. It's all too much."

I got up and went to look out the window, my back to her. Damned if I'd make it easy for her.

"You can build Speer's up again," Peg said to my back. "People will forget about the Duprée eventually. So will the police. Nobody can ruin a firm like Speer's in only one year—I know you'll find a way to build profits and regain Speer's good reputation. But it will take time, Earl. Maybe more time than I've got left. I went through the building process once—Amos Speer and I saw some pretty rough years before the galleries were established. I just don't think I could go through that again. I don't think I should have to."

Stony silence from me.

"I'll stay until you've found a new attorney, of course. I'll find one for you, if you like."

I looked out the window.

"Earl?"

I kept my back to her.

"Oh, Earl." I could hear the pain in her voice. "I was hoping you wouldn't take it this way. I wish you'd try to see what this means to me."

I said nothing.

"All right," she said in a resigned voice. "If that's the way you want it. I'll start looking for my successor."

I kept my back turned until I heard the door close behind her. Exit one meddling old crow, and good riddance.

If Amos Speer had had this trouble, Peg would have charged in and told him in no uncertain terms what he should do about it. But she'd had no suggestions for me at all. Maybe she was right—maybe it was just age catching up with her. The Peg McAllister who'd helped build Speer Galleries wasn't the defeated old woman who'd just left my office.

My pride had suffered a small blow, but that was nothing to the advantages gained. Of the three troublesome women in my life, two were gone or going and the third was out on a limb. Lieutenant D'Elia might be making threatening noises, but he was on a wild-goose chase. Money was the one real problem I had left; but as Peg said, nobody could ruin a firm as good as Speer's in only one year. (No, I didn't miss the implication that I'd made a good run at it.) Somehow Speer's would absorb the loss and slowly build up its profits again. It would take some doing, but we'd make it. I was sure we would. I was going to survive.

I knew I should leave well enough alone, but I couldn't resist. I punched out a number on the phone.

"Lieutenant D'Elia speaking."

"Find any six-hundred-thousand-dollar chairs lately, Lieutenant?" I gloated.

Silence.

"Oh, come now, Lieutenant, don't pout. Maybe you didn't look in the right places."

"We'll find it," he said grimly. "That chair has to be someplace. You might think you're safe because you've already sold it. Don't count on it."

"Well, keep looking. Anything's better than admitting you made a mistake," I said cheerfully and hung up.

Two days later I was reading a report from the new rare books expert at the London branch (prognosis: poor to fair) when the phone buzzed.

"Long distance on line two," my secretary said.
"Who is it?"
"Sorry, I didn't ask. Should I—?"
"Never mind, I'll take it." I punched the button. "Sommers."
"Right where he's supposed to be, nose to the grindstone and all that. Your conscientiousness is impressive, old chap. Of course, the new boy-type secretary could use a few basic pointers about screening callers. The June-bug told me all about him. She's just arrived here, by the way."
She didn't waste much time. "Glad to hear it, Wightman. You two deserve each other."
A whinny came over the line. "Enough chitchat—I call for a purpose. Perched on my scarred Gropius desk is a piece of porcelain you will be glad—nay, eager—to know about."
What gall. "You really think I would buy anything from you?"
"Who said anything about buying? Listen, dear boy, listen very carefully. Summon your fading cerebral faculties and concentrate. Try to visualize a graceful feminine figure, flowers in her hair, garbed in an exquisitely ornamented robe. She sits lightly atop a magnificent swan with powerful outstretched wings—"
Porcelain. A feminine figure. Sitting on a swan's back. I continued to hear a squawking in my ear but the words didn't mean anything.
"I say, old chap, you haven't gone and fainted, have you?"
I slammed down the receiver and rushed out of the office. The boy-type secretary said something as I rushed past but I didn't stop.
The traffic lights were against me; it took me forever to get to the Shadyside apartment. I unlocked the door, looked inside, then locked the door again. One glance was all I needed. The gaping hole in the fireplace wall told me what I wanted to know.

I went back to the gallery; I didn't have anywhere else to go. So June Murray had been willing to dirty her hands after all. She'd used the Leda to buy herself a partnership in Wightman's gallery.

Just when I was seeing light at the end of the tunnel. God damn Leonard Wightman to hell! *And* June. And god damn Nedda too—if she hadn't announced to the world that the Leda had been stolen at the time of Amos Speer's murder, those two vultures in San Francisco would never have realized the significance of the Meissen figurine.

June had noticed the patched brickwork. She'd dug out the Leda, and then probably spent a few minutes wondering why I would hide a porcelain figurine behind bricks and mortar. Then she'd remembered: something had been stolen from Amos Speer's house the day he was killed. She'd probably checked either with the police or the newspaper morgue; somehow I doubted that she'd called Nedda. When June realized she had evidence linking me to a murder, she'd probably taken a long time thinking over what to do. Blackmailers are in a notoriously high-stress, low-security profession. So she'd opted for safety in numbers and contacted Wightman, and now I'd have the two of them on my back for the rest of my life.

Or the rest of theirs. Leonard Wightman and June Murray. Under their thumbs forever?

Intolerable.

Therefore I would not tolerate it. *I would not*. I hadn't come this far just to knuckle under to those two. Wightman and his June-bug were going to have to go. And the Leda—well, this time the Leda would be smashed to smithereens.

I couldn't believe I'd been so foolish as to let a sentimental attachment to a piece of porcelain put me in this position. My trophy of survival? Hah! Utter stupidity. Unforgivable. Briefly the thought crossed my mind that keeping the Leda was a sign that I really wanted to be caught and punished. One of the first things you think of, I suppose. I dismissed the notion as fanciful; too much pop psychology in the air these days. I didn't want to be caught. I wasn't going to be caught. I *would* not be caught.

Once before I'd made up my mind to kill a man. I hadn't done it, but only because that man had managed to fade into the scenery. But I knew where these two were. Oh yes, I knew exactly where they were. For some reason I found myself thinking of Miss Centerfold, sitting behind the reception desk in Wightman's gallery. I wondered how long she'd last now that June Murray was out there. Wouldn't matter. Neither June nor Wightman would be around much longer themselves.

I'd pretend to go along with whatever they wanted. I'd have to remember to stay in character, to call Wightman *asshole* a few times. Just delay them long enough to make my plans. My real plans. I sat staring at the grain in the cherrywood table, waiting for their second call.

The phone ran instead of buzzing; I remembered my secretary hadn't been in the outer office when I got back. "Sommers."

"Earl? This is Charlie Bates. I gotta—"

"Charlie! My god, just the man I was thinking of! Charlie, I need to see you. Can we meet?"

"Sure, Earl. I—"

"The yak pens in an hour?"

"I'll be there," he promised.

I hung up, feeling excited and more alive than I'd felt once during this last long, horrible, depressing month. It was going to work—I knew it was going to work! Unless Charlie had been calling to tell me he'd changed professions again. But I didn't think so. No, it was all going to fall into place.

I wondered how much Charlie Bates charged for a double dip.

This time Charlie got there first. He was sitting on the bench, watching two of the yaks exchanging amorous glances. Charlie looked glum. Christ, not another suicidal period, I hoped. Not now.

He looked up and saw me. "Sit down, Earl. I got something to tell you."

I sat. "Can it wait? I've got something for *you*—"

"No, me first. I called you, remember? You better hear this."

"All right, but make it fast, will you?"

"It'll be fast. I got a new contract."

So what was that to me? "You're not going to tell me about it, are you?"

"Yeah, I am. You—"

"Wait a minute, Charlie—I don't want to hear this."

"Yes, you do. I owe you, Earl."

"Charlie—stop. I don't want to know."

"Earl, doncha understand? You're the mark."

"What?"

"The contract's on you, Earl."

I understood what he was saying. I knew what the words meant—we both spoke English. I stared at that murderous little creep and wondered what the hell he was talking about. The contract was on me, he said. Sure it was. On *me*. Charlie was watching me sadly.

"Me?" I finally said. "You accepted a contract on *me?*"

"Yeah, Earl."

"I'm your next victim?"

He made a face at the word. "That's about it."

"Your old b-b-buddy Earl?" I was so angry and horrified and sick I couldn't talk straight. "Your oldest friend? That you're so grateful to?"

"But I am grateful, Earl. Why d'you think I'm telling you about it? Because I owe you. This way you'll have a chance."

"A chance to do what? Run and hide?"

"Better'n no chance at all."

"Charlie, why didn't you refuse the contract? You know I'd make up the fee."

"Wouldn't solve nothing, Earl. If I don't take the contract, somebody else does. With me, at least, you know what's happening. You know who to look out for. Nobody else is gonna warn you."

I didn't say anything for a minute, trying to get my breathing under control, trying to come to grips with this grotesque new reality that had just been thrust at me. Charlie Bates was going to kill me. "You wouldn't be warning me yourself if you weren't sure you'd get me."

A look of simpering modesty, the blockhead. "Don't like to brag, but I am good at my work."

His work. "Funny way to pay me back, Charlie. By killing me."

"Aw, that's business, Earl. That don't have nothing to do with me and you."

Business as usual. That cretin had worked it out in his so-called mind that if he *warned* me before he went ahead and killed me, that would somehow make everything all right. His debt would be paid, the scales would be balanced, it would all even out. That's the way he thought. That's really the way he thought.

"Charlie, look. I'll leave town. I'll give up the galleries, I'll just disappear. I can do that—you did it yourself, you know it can be done. Say you couldn't find me . . ."

He shook his head. "Won't work, Earl. *Somebody*'ll find you."

"All right then, say you did it. Say you found me and killed me and my, my body—say it's in the river. Say I was crossing a bridge and you shot me and I fell into the river."

"Guard rails too high."

"Then something else! It doesn't matter what—we can work out the details! Charlie, I'll pay you double, triple what you're getting—anything! Name your price—it's yours."

Charlie looked offended. "Wish you hadna said that. I don't take bribes. A man's gotta have pride in his work. This is my calling, Earl—it ain't just another job. Besides, you don't play favorites in this business and stay in this business."

I still couldn't believe it, I just couldn't believe what I was hearing. "You're talking about business ethics when you're planning to *kill* me?"

"Shh! Keep your voice down."

I'd heard the edge of hysteria in my own voice. "Charlie, what do you want? Name it. There must be something you don't have that I can get for you."

"Don't do this, Earl."

"Something, Charlie! Think. What do you want that you don't have?"

"I got all I want."

"All you have to do is tell me. I'll get it for you, I don't care what it is—*Charlie, I'll get you your own yak!* Would you like that? I can do it, I can arrange it!"

He turned his head away from me in embarrassment. "Listen at yourself, Earl. You're babbling."

You're babbling. With those two words Charlie told me in a way I couldn't possibly misunderstand that I didn't have a chance in hell of talking him out of it. How many times in the past twenty years had I told Charlie Bates to stop babbling? And now I was the one who was doing it, and Charlie Bates was embarrassed.

We sat without talking for a while. The yaks had all moved to the far side of the pen; I kept staring at the large pile of droppings one of them had left as a calling card.

Finally I roused myself. "How long do I have?"

"Twenty-four hours." He gave a humorless laugh. "I sound like the sheriff in a western. It ain't much, Earl, and I'm sorry about that. But twenty-four hours is all the head start I can give you."

I stood up, feeling several hundred years old. One more thing. "Charlie."

"Yeah, Earl?"

"It was my wife who hired you, of course."

He looked at me sadly. "Yeah, Earl."

Twenty-four hours.

My first thought was to find Nedda, to make her understand that if she didn't call off the contract I was going to kill her right then and there. But Nedda had gone to New York—removing herself from the scene of the crime. The scene of the crime! Christ. Nedda had probably taken Arthur Simms along to help establish her alibi—I wondered if she'd informed him of that little detail before they took off.

No: Nedda had only said she was going to New York. She could be anywhere—Caracas, Antwerp, Bombay, any place her passport and her credit cards could take her. New York was the one place she wouldn't be. Forget Nedda.

My second thought was to call Valentine, to arrange for a round-the-clock bodyguard. But even as I was thinking it, I saw how futile it would ultimately be. How alert can a bodyguard stay forever? All it'd take would be one moment of inattention on the part of any one of the guards—and Charlie Bates would earn his fee. There really is no way to protect yourself from someone who's determined to get you. I wondered how much Charlie was charging Nedda. What was my life worth on the old buddy scale of values?

My third thought brought the taste of bile to my mouth. But this was no time to be choosy. I went to the police.

Lieutenant D'Elia listened to my edited story with an attention that would have been flattering under other circumstances. "Let me get this straight," he said. "This hit man *warned* you he's going to kill you?"

"That's right. You see, I know him personally—we went to school together. We were friends once."

"And that's why he warned you?"

"I think it's a point of pride with him. Not sneaking up on an old friend, I mean. He's a peculiar man."

"I'll say. You say his name is Bates?"

"Charlie Bates. But he must be going by a different name now."

"Which is?"

"How would I know? I don't even know how to get in touch with him."

"Well then, if you don't know the name he's using and you don't have a picture—"

"But can't you find out what name he's using? Don't you have ways of handling these things?"

"Within limits. You can look at the mug shots—"

"That won't do any good. Charlie's never been arrested."

"You seem to know a lot about him."

"I've known him for twenty years! Up until about a year ago, when he just dropped out of sight. I guess that's when he became a hit man."

"A year ago?" D'Elia said alertly. "About the time Amos Speer was murdered?"

I was just too discouraged to care. "About then. I'm not really sure."

"Did you hire him to kill Speer?"

Variation on the same old tune. "No, Lieutenant, I've never hired Charlie Bates to kill anyone."

"Who hired him to kill you?"

"My wife."

"How do you know?"

"Charlie told me."

D'Elia's eyebrows went up. "This guy's the most accommodating hit man I've ever come across. He just told you?"

"He's not the brightest man in the world. It probably didn't even occur to him I'd go to the police."

"Now that's something I find very odd indeed. Why would he feel so sure you wouldn't go to the police?"

Thin ice, thin ice. "I told you he wasn't very bright. Lieutenant, we're wasting time—he gave me only twenty-four hours."

"Why does your wife want you dead?"

This part of it I could tell. "She wants a divorce, I want the galleries, neither one of us will give in."

"And that's her way of solving domestic problems? By hiring a contract killer?"

"Nedda doesn't like it when she doesn't get her own way." *Cause them trouble, cause them both trouble*. "She has a lover—a man named Arthur Simms, with Keystone Management. He's probably in on it."

D'Elia wrote down the name. "Well, we'll look into it."

"You'll look into it? What does that mean?"

"We'll have a talk with Mrs. Sommers—"

"She's not here—she left town. So she'd be out of the way when it happens."

"When she gets back, then."

"For Christ's sake, I'll be *dead* by the time she gets back! What good'll that do me?"

"Look, about all we can do now is put out an APB on Bates, based on the description you gave me. But frankly, Sommers, he sounds just like a hundred other guys I know. We might be able to pick him up, but don't hold your breath. Then if we do manage to find him, all we can do is bring him in for questioning. We can't charge him, since no crime has been committed—"

"He killed Amos Speer!" I blurted out.

D'Elia leaned back in his chair and looked at me from under half-closed lids.

"I, I think he killed him," I stammered helplessly. "I'm sure of it. I'm sure he did. I think Nedda hired him that time too."

D'Elia merely said, "Oh?"

"Well, it makes sense, doesn't it?" I heard my voice rising with desperation. "If she could hire a killer to get rid of one husband, why couldn't she have done it with the other one too? You can charge him with suspicion for Speer's murder, can't you?"

"On what evidence? All I have is your say-so. And you're just guessing."

A squirrel cage, I was in a squirrel cage. "You can hold him for a while without charging him, I know you can do that. You can do that, can't you? Just hold him for questioning?"

"Yes, we can do that."

"Then why aren't you doing it?" I was yelling. "Why do you just sit there with that smug look on your face"?"

"Relax, Sommers. We'll keep an eye out for your Mr. Bates."

"You'll keep an eye out for him! Is that all? D'Elia, are you just going to sit there and let Charlie Bates kill me?"

He didn't say a word. He lowered his eyelids all the way shut and after a moment raised them again. There was something ominously close to being a gleam in his eye. One corner of his mouth twitched.

"My god," I said slowly, at last understanding. "That's what you're going to do. That's exactly what you're going to do!"

D'Elia hadn't believed my impulsive lie about Nedda hiring Charlie to kill Speer; he was still convinced I was behind it. But he knew he wasn't going to be able to prove it any more than he'd been able to find traces of an illegal sale of a genuine Duprée. He knew he couldn't get me himself, so he was quite willing to sit back and let Charlie Bates take care of it for him. He was going to do that. This upstanding upholder of the law was really going to do that. This wasn't the ending he'd planned on, but he'd take it. Lieutenant D'Elia was not at all displeased with the way things were working out, and he wasn't making the slightest effort to hide it.

"My god," I said dully, "what am I going to do?"

D'Elia smiled at me benignly. "Have you thought of taking a long vacation?"

My fourth thought was to run.

15

Run where?

I was afraid to use my passport—wouldn't that leave a trail for Charlie to follow? I didn't know how big an organization he was hooked up with, I didn't know what kind of information they had access to. But he free-lanced for the mob now, and those guys could find out everything they ever wanted to know about everything. But killing me wasn't a mob contract—it was a private deal. Oh hell, I didn't know.

Without a passport I could still go to Mexico or Canada. But Mexico was out; one gringo living in a Mexican village would stand out like a sore thumb. Possibly some remote spot in Canada? Where they don't speak French?

I decided against it. It is my considered opinion that most people forced to go into hiding would head for some isolated place where they think their pursuers would be unlikely to seek them. Some distant spot, too small to be on the map, too out-of-the-way for anyone to stumble on it by chance. *I'll be safe here*, that's what they'd think. Most people, yes, that's what they'd think.

I am firmly convinced this is a mistake, yes I am. You have to be sneaky, you have to think the way they think you'll think and then turn around and think the other way. My old buddy Charlie knew I was running and he'd think I'd want to put as much real estate between me and him as I could. Hide on an island in Canada or on a mesa in Arizona or in a swamp in Florida or someplace with not many folks around to tell tales. That's what he'd think I was thinking.

But Charlie's dumb, he always thinks the obvious things. Strangers are noticed in sparsely populated areas, outsiders can't help but call attention to themselves. Even if you could sneak in late at night when no one was looking, you still had to have food and that meant contact with other people. Those faraway places with the strange-sounding names can be death traps.

So the only answer was the purloined letter bit. Bury yourself among hordes of people, make yourself look like them, get lost in the crowd.

I decided on New York. It was close and I was running out of time. I bought a ticket under a false name and crowded in between a fat priest and a sari-wrapped Indian woman in the tourist section.

Nedda, Nedda, Nedda. You were my enemy all along. Not Speer or Wightman or D'Elia. Not even Peg or June. Just you, Nedda, my modest and loving wife. With you on my side I could have licked them all, sob sob. Most spoiled children just ignore the toys they tire of, but you—you have to destroy yours. What if I hadn't sent Charlie to kill old Amos? If I'd just waited, would you have taken care of him yourself? And how long before you dethrone King Arthur, you treacherous Guinevere? Selfish, greedy Nedda. All your life you've had everything you wanted. You don't even know what it's like to do without. You're stupid, Nedda. You don't know nothing.

New York, New York, it's a wonderful town.

I found a place in the West Village and moved in with the cockroaches and the hooker down the hall and the brothers shooting up on the stairway and the drunks peeing in the vestibule. I locked myself in my room and right away I start wishing I have a gun. Or a knife or a baseball bat or something to defend myself with. But I can't go out looking for no weapon—what if I bump into Charlie on the street corner? Will he snuff me right there? Will he say *Hi, buddy, gladaseeya* before he lets me have it? I have to go out sometime, a guy hiding in his room all day every day is gonna draw attention to hisself and I don't want to do that and I don't know what to do. Just a few days, thass all I need, until my beard grows out and my clothes gets grubby and I start to looking like everybody else around here. All I need is a little time. Some kid I'm paying to go get groceries, he's the only one knows I'm here but kids talk and I ain't really safe yet.

So I sit by my one window looking out over Charles Street and watching everybody that passes by, thass all I do. Watching for Charlie on Charles Street. Good old Charlie Bates. My buddy. *Earl, you're the only friend I ever had,* whine whine whine. If I'da just said *Piss off, Charlie,* I wouldn't be hiding in this dump now. Friendship, ain't it wonderful.

Charlie and Nedda, what a pair. How'd she do it? How'd that mattressback find out about Charlie? I remember, I remember she tole him to call her when he got back from one of his jobs, one of them see-what-a-man-I-am jobs he likes so pissing much. But I laid down the law, I did, I tole her I dint want Charlie Bates in my house, she understood that. So what's she do, she asks him over anyways, sometime I'm not there, for lunch maybe at first, thass it. She thinks it's funny, sneaking Charlie in behind my back, thass just the kinda thing she does for kickies. I wonder did they sleep together? Naw, even Nedda wouldn't go to bed with Charlie Bates. I make a picture in my head of Nedda and Charlie screwing away and I laugh out loud it's so funny.

So then what happens? She tells him my husband he don't understand me, it's so sad, I got nobody to turn to. Wisht I knew a strong man to help poor little me, yeah, thass the line she'd use. And dumb old Charlie he'd eat it right up, big comic book hero saving the helpless broad. Helpless my ass. Like, like that Italian bitch way back when that kept getting rid of her lovers, by putting poison on her lips.

Or maybe it dint go that way. Maybe she saw through him right off, maybe she said can you give me a name, somebody to do a job for me. And he gave her a name all right, his name, his own, and the deal's made. I shoulda knew they'd get together, my best friend and my loving wife, happens on tee vee alla time.

Nedda I understand, she's like that, nobody's important to her besides herself I mean. But Charlie, Charlie don't have no call going after me, not even for money not even especially for money. Charlie he's my best friend and a man don't go around putting holes in his best friend. He shouldna took the contract, he shoulda just pulled out that old automatic and popped Nedda one two three just like that. Thass what friends do. They help. Alla times I helped him, giving him math answers, writing his book reports for him and remembering to spell a word wrong now and then so the teach wouldn't suspect nothing. He owes me.

He owes me a helluva lot, come to think of it. I got him outa scrapes, I was always there when he needed me. One time in school there was this big black dude went around taking money off people. He always had three or four other dudes with him so there wasn't nothing to do except hand it over. One day I have twenty-five cents in my pocket, my last quarter, two bits to my name. This dude says if I don't give it to him he's gonna break my head for me. So I give it to him, my last two bits. Now when you get ripped off to the tune of ten bucks, well thass crime and you gotta live with crime these days. But when a guy takes your last quarter just to show you he can do it, he's only doing it to make you feel small. I couldn't let him get away with that no sir.

So I tell Charlie to break his arm and Charlie done it. Then you know what that six-foot black musclehead does? He goes home and tells his momma. And his momma she calls the school principal and the principal calls in Charlie and all hell breaks loose. Charlie don't talk so good and this principal he don't want to listen nohow, he don't wanta hear nothing about no dudes taking money off other guys. So I goes in and I says the whole thing was a accident, I seen it all. I got this guy with all his college degrees believing his black dude tripped and Charlie threw out an arm to help him and the dude goes down thinking Charlie hit him. This smartass principal ends up *apologizing* to Charlie.

And Charlie's hanging on to me and saying *Earl you're the best friend a guy could ever have* and all that shit and I tell him to go break the dude's other arm and he done it. And this time the dude he don't go crying to his momma, he got the message this time. None of them dudes bothered us after that. And Charlie's dancing around and calling me buddy and thanking me for making everything work out. Charlie wouldna made it through school without me helping him along.

But that ain't nothing, the real thing he oughta remember is I saved his life. He was wanting to die and he woulda gone on and popped his own cork if it hadna been for me. I stopped him, I made things easier I put the gun in his hand. I shown him a way to go on living and be a big man and live good and, and, and I saved *his* life. He should oughta save mine. Fair's fair. He owes me. Why, if I hadna sent him out to get old Amos Speer, Charlie Bates would be dead hisself right now.

Charlie'd be dead and Speer'd still be alive and still married to that bitch and she wouldn't have no need to send Charlie after me. Goddam you Amos Speer I hope you're roasting in hell. You old cocksucker if you'da just give me a partnership when I needed it none of this woulda happened, it's your own fault you're dead you shoulda cut me in.

The kid I'm paying to get stuff for me come in for a minute. I send him to get groceries, much as he can carry and then not come back for a coupla days. He don't need to come ever day, just oncet in a while.

But if Charlie Bates gets me, I'm gonna get him too. I won't be around to see it, but it's gonna happen. Goddam fucking right it's gonna happen. Lieutenant D'Elia, he'll take care of it for me. I tole him, I tole him all about it dint I? I give him Charlie's name and said it clear how Nedda hired him and D'Elia he's gonna get them both, he won't let them get away with it. He'll even get the lover boy, whatsisname, Arthur something. D'Elia's a good man, he cares about the law, he likes catching people he'll find a way he's tricky. He's got three of them to go after now, he's gonna have a fine old time playing good guy tracking down the baddies. He'll do it, he'll do it, he almost got me dint he? You gotta have faith in something I believe in Lieutenant D'Elia he's a good man, he'll get them.

Charlie and Nedda don't know I tole him. They think they're safe, aint *they* in for a surprise! Shit, I wisht I could see it, how I'd love to see their faces when he tells them he knows. Nedda don't like having police around, it don't look right, too bad cookie you shoulda thought of that. Charlie's gonna be harder, he knows how to disappear but he don't know they'll be waiting on him when he gets back. He'll go back to Pittsburgh for sure, he don't know no place else. I shoulda tole Valentine afore I left yeah the two of them together, Valentine and D'Elia what a team, they'll get them Valentine's smart he can help D'Elia—

Where's the goddam kid with my groceries? I'm hungry and I gotta keep my strength up. I'm thinking something that makes me laugh. Those two bloodsuckers out in San Frisco if I die they ain't gonna get nothing. *Nothing!* Out, in, the, cold. Freeze your ass Whiteman. And the broad too—April? I can get *all* my enemies just by dying thass all I have to do.

There's the kid but he ain't carrying nothing where's my groceries? He said he'd get them he promised. Looka him walking along the street big as life talking to that guy like he don't have nothing better to do. I gotta eat fore Charlie gets here and he stands there talking to that guy and pointing—

God. Oh god.

He's here.